Shade of Angels

DATE DUE

By William Clar

MY 2 9 78		
F 05 78		

PRINTED IN U.S.A.

D1366450

The moral right of the author has been asserted.

The characters and events portrayed in this book are fictitious. Any similarity to real person, living or dead, is coincidental and not intended by the author.

Forward

There is way too much water under the bridge, to coin a phrase, as it pertains to my age. This book is an observation on some of that fast moving water. The lines for things we hoped for and things we need start to get very clear around this time of life. We don't move as fast, laugh as loud, or pass judgment as quickly as we once did. Things that were set in stone in our minds ten years ago have long since been uprooted, leaving an openness and a cautious awareness that something was here and it was probably wrong. At this age you need to start getting all the beliefs and smooth rocks of the soul lined up. You need to start believing in something, anything that will move you on.

This story moves me on, maybe not a long way down the path, but far enough to see some new ground and a few more miles of open road. **Shade of Angels**- a great title for the rest of my time on this rock.

William Clark/2014

The legionnaire sergeant gathered his men, his face drawn, solemn. "Men, I have bad news and good news. Which would you like to hear first?"

"Bad news first!" shouted one of the men.

The sergeant cleared his throat. "Okay. Men, we are surrounded."

The men were silent, and then one shouted out. "Well, what's the good news?"

The sergeant smiled broadly. "The good news is that we can now shoot in any direction."

Shade of Angels

By

William Clark

Table of Contents

Chapter One

Sometimes you let go of the important things, things that can no longer be sustained. Words are said with feeling, sometimes wrapped in tears that hit harder than any bullet. You never recover from those kinds of hits to the heart. You bleed inside until you're dry. The cold wind of loss and razor-sharp reality take over at some later time, and you know right down to your bones that something once precious and beautiful is dead. It now lives in the dark places of memory, the bedrock of the soul, in places where you seldom venture for the risk of more pain.

Jim Cross was caught in a moment of haunting memory as he watched his dogs excitedly chase the ball he had kicked half-heartedly. Standing in the cold, muted sunlight of late February, a chill ran down his back as he looked at the letter again, hoping against hope that he had read it wrong the first time. He was being denied unemployment for the second time in the last eight months.

Because he had quit his last position instead of being fired, he was not eligible for any type of assistance. Yet he knew, that if he hadn't quit he would have assaulted the supervisor who had seemed determined to make his life miserable just for the fun of it. At the moment he quit, walking away from a ninety thousand dollars a year job had seemed a whole lot better than going to jail for punching the living shit out of some guy. He crumpled the letter and stuffed it into his pocket, knowing even that was a lie.

He wouldn't have fought the guy. He probably wouldn't have even said a word when the axe came down. No, this would have been a bloodless killing. The company wanted him fired and had sent the new guy in to make it happen. Over a short period of time he had gone from golden boy to pariah; his services and presence were no longer needed at the company. In their minds he was out of date, out of step, and needed to be out the door as soon as possible.

He had seen it coming. He had been handed more and more mandates and requirements that could not be met on incredibly short time lines that were impossible to meet. The commands, all delivered through the phone with a passive aggressive tone, only amplified the pressure. The snippy e-mails, the barely controlled threats of termination on a daily basis did what they were intended to do. They drove him out of the job he had loved, a position he had waited for most of his career.

Now, for the first time in his 60 years on the planet he was totally dependent on someone else to take care of him financially. His wife, a woman who had fallen out of love with him, had a good job that paid the rent and kept food on the table. He had seen the warm light in her eyes slowly dim and then disappear altogether when he had been unable to find work over the last several months. Now, she barely tolerated his existence.

The last months had been full of disappointments. He had sent hundreds of resumes, made hundreds of phone calls, but still had received nothing but polite statements and vacuous e-mails either notifying him that they had accepted another candidate or that he was over-qualified for the position.

Each denial, every failed submission had driven a long, cold emotional nail into the coffin of his marriage. He was no longer a provider, no longer the strong man who waded into the challenges of his work with the self-assurance that he could solve any problem. Those days were long gone. Now, he stood in his back yard, a beaten warrior, weaponless and wounded by those things he once controlled but couldn't control any longer.

One of the Shepherds trotted up, dropped the dirty tennis ball at his feet and then looked at him with an excited expression, waiting for it to be thrown or kicked again, an expression that said, "You need to do this. You need to play with this ball. I brought this back to you. Now you do your part."

He tossed the ball and watched as both dogs ran full out across the yard and then over the small embankment that marked the end of his property. Total abandonment to the task, he thought smiling. The only thing that existed in their lives was the pursuit of that dirty, worn-out tennis ball that had lain out in the front yard under the snow all those winter months. Total commitment was something he had once believed in, something he had anchored his soul to that allowed him to get through life. His job had failed him. Some of the failure he blamed on himself.

He always thought of his ability to see the hits coming as one of his strong points. Seeing the bad guy coming through the wire with real death in his heart was something he thought he would always be able to see at a distance. His ability to escape to fight another day had been taken for granted.

Commitment to the cause, wherever that mantra took him, was what he had lived by so many years ago. And, now, standing in the back yard, with eighteen dollars in his pocket and even less in his bank account, he was taking serious stock of how he had ended up this way. The only thing of any real value he had left was the love of his two dogs and the new Sig Saur 45 caliber pistol he wore under his coat. He had bought it a month ago and had used it last night.

The last thing on his mind as he had carried the new gun out of the local gun store that night was that he could be involved in a deadly shooting that would take the lives of two people. One of the men he had only met twice. The other was a complete stranger, a homicidal gift from the bad side of town.

The stranger had stepped from the shadows shooting towards his car, the rounds going high and left, hitting the back wall of the abandoned gas station Cross had been using in most of his business.

Cross had recognized the second man as he had come up with a pistol from under his driver's seat and fired at nearly point blank range, his round blowing the stuffing out of Cross's headrest, filling the cold air between them with white foam confetti. The bullet had missed by millimeters giving Cross a chance to draw and fire his weapon hitting the shooter's left eye from less than two feet away. The 45-caliber slug had taken the entire back half of the man's skull with it as it punched out the back passenger side window.

The first attacker had fallen over his own feet in haste and tumbled headlong into Cross's closed passenger side door. His clumsiness had provided ample seconds of distraction, precious moments that had given Cross the ability to shoot through the door, both rounds finding their mark blowing large ragged holes through the man's neck and jaw. He had bled out in less than a minute.

The traffic that night had been busy. A light rain had begun to fall just before dark, adding a deeper, natural hush to the already rain soaked streets. He had been doing business on the bad side of town for the last month, a profitable, but highly dangerous routine. He knew being an older white guy in this part of Detroit after dark was just asking for trouble. It was amazing how hard and far desperation could drive a man.

The shooting was spilt milk in his mind. He was way past feeling sorry for himself. He had crossed over the second that black son-of-a-bitch tried to rip him off and kill him in that alley. Like most guys of his generation, he didn't dislike blacks as a race but carried a cautious awareness whenever he was around them, especially young black males because he could see the disdain in their eyes, their barely controlled anger in his presence.

Living in Detroit he had daily contacts with blacks. Most of the bus drivers, police officers, store clerks, and mailmen were black, and he had gotten along fine with them over the years. Now, after the shooting, he looked at them differently. He recognized a paranoia that he could do little to control.

His slide in life from working as a security consultant worldwide to marijuana dealer had only taken three years. He had convinced himself of the nobility of his actions. He had looked into the cold, impassive face of failure and decided that he was not going to blink, no way, no hearts and flowers dirge about the unfairness of it all. No, he was taking this trip on his own ticket. He was tired of playing by the rules, tired of eating the leftovers from other people's dreams. Good, bad, or deadly, this was going to play out the way he wanted it.

As far as the two mouth-breathers in the alley, life's a bitch. They would not be missed. The last suspect on the Heat's roster would be a senior citizen white guy who had no attachment to the dead whatsoever. The only thing he had left at the scene was blood and dead bodies. To hell with them and to hell with anybody else that tried the same shit. He had a lethal skill set, something years of law enforcement and civilian tactical ranges had given him. Kill houses, static ranges, and movement to contact drills had given him a fine edge when it came to armed conflict. Handgun, long gun, shot gun, assault rifles were all familiar tools in the toolbox.

Heading back into the house with the Shepherds close behind, he shook off the last of the self-pity and remorse for how things had gone the night before. The wife hadn't even noticed the damage to her car. The two small crown-shaped bullet holes at the bottom of the passenger door had escaped detection. He would pound them flat in the morning and forget about the whole thing.

For now he had to check on his plants and start breaking down the two pounds of Holy Ghost weed he had in his safe. He had to find some new customers and a new distributor. Killing the help was no way to run a business. "Cowboy-up, buckaroo," he told himself. This was something he had chosen. Now all he had to do was hang on and see it through. He passed his wife in the hallway on his way up to get a shower. "Hey."

"Hey," she replied walking past. That was the extent of the conversation, pretty much par for the course lately.

"So, I guess sex is out?" he shouted down from the stairs.

"What do you think? I am really tired tonight," she replied. "Maybe this weekend."

He walked into the bathroom without answering, remembering a time when they could not get enough of each other. Yeah, maybe this weekend, he thought, laying his pistol on the edge of the sink. Hell, pigs just might learn how to fly also.

He let the hot water blast the soreness in his neck and wash away the tiny blood specks that had sprinkled his face and hair. As he looked at his bare feet he was surprised at how deeply colored the red stained water was as it circled the drain. He snorted a laugh. It just showed him how iced-over her indifference really was. He was covered in someone else's blood and she hadn't even noticed. Yeah, maybe this weekend. He wouldn't hold his breath.

***

Jeff Kitchens had his own problems when it came to work. He had way too much of it. There were six open cases on his desk right now, and Captain Taylor had just made him the lead on two more. He was working twelve hours a day, six days a week and was falling more behind every hour. He had been with homicide for the last seven years and in all that time had never seen the murder rate this high. The bangers and the dope slingers were killing each other wholesale.

A year ago the city had gone bankrupt making the evening news around the rest of the country. To the few remaining families on Mack Avenue where the bodies fell, bankruptcy, nightly gunfire, and regular random death were old news. Been that way for years, and it didn't matter how much heat was put on the street from city hall. In this part of town, like a lot of places where the shot-callers got tired of caring and throwing money at the problems, they let the crippled wolves and crazy-brave take over.

Your skin color would not save you here. Black on black crime was a staple. Survival depended on chance and how fast you reacted to the bad shadows. Kids, the elderly, women, and anyone else who just happened to be in the way were all potential targets. Kitchens had been a beat-cop for ten years in the area before he went to Dicks, but it had been a different Detroit in those days.

Big auto was already on life support, but enough people had decent paying jobs that the community kept breathing. In the summer, ice cream trucks patrolled the neighborhoods, giving the people of the well-worn area a semblance of the American dream.

Now, most of the houses were empty, abandoned, occupied by the ragged ghosts of what could have been. For Kitchens it was a heartbreaking reality he faced on a daily basis. He knew most of the people who had lived in those abandoned homes. He had watched as more than he could count buried their dead and then buried their dreams of anything better.

Even when he wasn't answering a call in the neighborhood, he still couldn't shake the bad vibe of moving through a crime scene whenever he drove through. Today two more murders had been dropped on his plate. As he stood in the cold, early morning light looking at the scene, the familiar sickness of the soul started to rise in his gut.

Both men had died bloody. A heavy-caliber round had scattered blood, bone, and tissue of the one in the car all over the back seat and rear window. The one on the ground had taken two in the neck and jaw, nearly severing the head from the body, a bad way to go in anybody's book.

The ME arrived moments later and with a tired precision started taking photos of the bodies. "You got IDs on these two?" he asked, taking several more camera shots.

Kitchens shoved his hands deep in his coat pockets shivering from the cold. "Not yet, I didn't want to roll them until you got what you needed. You ready?"

The elderly medical examiner nodded. "Yeah, I'm about to freeze out here."

Kitchens pulled the wallet from the man on the ground. "Let's see, ah, this is a Desmond Moss, DOB 6/15/86. That makes him what, 28?" He stuffed the wallet into a small plastic bag and then handed the driver's license to the ME. "After you log him in, Doc, I'll run these guys off the IDs. Bet you a shiny new dime we've had contact with them before."

The ME grunted a response as he rolled the body onto his back. "Looks like a large caliber round did all this damage," he announced, bending down close to the body. "I'd say a 45, maybe bigger."

A uniformed officer walked up beside Kitchens, holding a large roll of yellow police tape. "How much of this alley do you want marked off?" he asked as he tilted his head to look at the corpse. "Hey, you know what? I know this guy."

Kitchens knelt down next to the body and picked up the pistol with his gloved hand. "His ID says he's Desmond Moss. How do you know him?" The uniform held open the plastic bag as Kitchens dropped the gun in.

"I took him down on a domestic sometime last month. He beat the crap out of his girlfriend. I think they have a kid together. Real asshole. Took three of us to get him into my car. Fought us the whole way. I think his street name is Kojack."

Kitchens went through the rest of the man's pockets coming up with a wad of bills soaked in urine and blood and an extra loaded magazine of 9mm bullets. He dropped the rest of the man's property into the bag.

"Well, looks like ol' Kojack here ran into someone a whole lot tougher." He looked down the alley to the now busy street. "Tell you what, go ahead and block off both ends of the alley. That should be good enough. I doubt there is going to be much to find."

The ME opened the car door where the second victim lay slumped across the front seat.

"Hang on, Doc, let me give you a hand," announced Kitchens.

"Jesus, what a mess," mumbled the ME taking several photos of the body. "From the looks of it, this one took it right in the face. The back of his head is in the back seat."

Kitchen's pulled the wallet from the man's pants. "Okay, this is James Holloway. DOB 4/16/79. That makes him 35." He looked back at the body on the ground. "It's kind of strange that these two would be running together."

The ME stepped back from the car taking several more pictures. "Why's that?" he asked.

"Their ages. They're almost ten years apart. The young bloods rarely run with some OG."

The ME helped zip the body bags as several more assistants walked up to load the bags on stretchers.

"I should have the Tox and the rest of the forensics on these two by the middle of next week," replied the ME, peeling off his gloves and tossing them into one of the crime scene bags. "I'm not expecting any surprises."

Kitchens added his gloves to the bag. "That's fine, Doc. I'll check in with you later."

The ME grunted his customary response and walked back to his car. He needed coffee. His back hurt from lifting the dead. "God," he thought slumping in behind the wheel of his car, "I'm getting way to old for this shit first thing in the morning, way to old."

***

The daily mental exercise of introspection was starting to wear thin for Cross. The constant question of "what if" had become an uncomfortable drone in his waking hours. A haunting, sick-to-the-stomach kind of feeling was blocking his highs and deepening his lows and this weight anchoring his emotions seemed to grow heavier everyday. Food, sex, and even the thought of getting free from it all, all did little to ease the nagging trepidation and growing fear. And now he was a killer. Even though the act itself had been self-defense, he knew this self-rationalization would grow less effective as time wore on. The right thing to do, of course, was to drive down to the police station and turn himself in, walk up to the counter, drop his brand new pistol on top and tell whoever was there at the time the whole seedy story, let them know in grinding detail how growing marijuana in his home had started more out of desperation than anything else, how he had been unable to find work when he turned sixty and yet the house payment and car payments just kept on coming. The bank didn't care how old you were; they wanted their money and "by-God" you'd better not be late with that payment! A personal crisis meant nothing to them. You paid or you moved out. Period.

He would stand there, facing a stranger and tell them how he had watched the deep embers of love slowly fade in his wife's eyes, how she had lost respect for him, how he feared she would run out of any last compassion for his situation or concern for what would happen to him if she wasn't there to support him. How he felt she was tolerating his presence only until she could find the will and the courage to ask for a divorce.

He would spill it all to the stranger with a badge, hoping against hope that they would understand that he had been a unable to stop the slide, powerless to fight the dark circumstances he now found himself facing. He would stand there, shaking more from adrenalin than fear, instinctively knowing what would happen next. They would not understand. A detective would be called. Rights would be read, and his life as a troubled, yet free, man would be over.

They would write in their notebooks, record him as he retold his story of desperation and then put him in a cell. He would become "property," a number in the system that would soon be forgotten - fed, clothed and housed at the discretion of others, the ultimate loss of control in an institutional hell.

He shook the images from his head and rinsed off the shaving razor. He liked the goatee; it gave him a hard look that he now, for unknown reasons, wanted to portray. His look kept people at a distance, made them think twice about pushing the issue. To move people out of the way without saying a word was power, something he desperately needed.

The face he now saw in the mirror was that of a man who had once been on the inside of the government machine, one of the cool guys with the expense account, the government clearance and the priceless nonchalance as if it would always be that way. "Yeah, one of those guys," he whispered to the image, "one of those guys."

Chapter Two

The decision for intervention had been in the works for months, even years. The measurement of man, the yardstick from now to the inevitable end, would be conducted the way it had always been. The full weight and measure of blunt and sometimes brutal honesty would be by the rules as they had always applied.

When the Messenger allowed himself to think about the process, he was motivated to even greater heights to "get it right." The message had been sent, received and now action was called for. If he felt joy in anything he did within his current existence, the intervention into the lives of one of "them" was one of the best things he did.

He admired their courage, the strength it took to survive their lives. He had seen thousands die, maybe a million, and yet they continued to move on, progress through adversity, fight for that last moment of life in this reality. The human spirit, in all of its terrible beauty, played out everyday, every moment - truly awe-inspiring. It was something that made them easy to care for.

He always looked forward to the first encounter. He would be on their time, a radical change from where he normally existed. They had invented the progression of time, a way of marking the moments and seasons of their lives. In his reality, time was only measured by events, the things fragile man did or didn't do that made things happen in their framework of consciousness.

He was a solider, as he had always been, a veteran of many thunderous battles, wars that had shaken the very foundations of heaven. He had led legions against the other side and had prevailed every time.

Now, his task was to influence one man, adjust a behavior, to prevent a greater wound. A soldier of the first order, he would obey without question or thought.

The Messenger's appearance in these individual lives was always met with stunned disbelief, tears of fear, regret, and shock. They would cry for forgiveness, wail at his feet for mercy, terrified by the very idea of what he stood for, but he was neither touched nor swayed by their pleas. His instructions were clear and his allegiance unwavering to a power beyond comprehension, the final authority controlling all of the actions.

Eventually, most would calm and submit to the correction. In rare cases some would challenge the instructions, fighting the new course of action with an unreasonable will bordering on insanity. These cases had to be handled very carefully.

The Messenger suspected that Cross might be one of those men. Tough and resolute in conviction, solid and resilient in adversity, all admirable traits in a man, except when those very traits could lead to doom.

By eight that morning an introduction into the life of James Edward Cross would take place and that introduction would change everything.

***

"I have been having strange dreams lately," he said, pouring his morning coffee. He sat down at the small dining room table, still groggy from the poor night's sleep. His wife of ten years sat on the couch watching the morning news, still in her pajamas.

"Did you say something?" she asked, lighting a cigarette. He hated it when she smoked in the house. She had been smoking outside to please him but had stopped even that courtesy months ago. There had been hundreds of arguments about it but now he didn't even bother to say anything.

They had both been up since seven but met in the kitchen. This wasn't a product of their recent tension. They had been sleeping in separate rooms for years out of a need to get better rest.

"I said I'm having weird dreams."

She blew a long, steady stream of smoke to the ceiling. "You stay up too late. That's the problem."

"Maybe, but the dreams are really strange, stranger than normal."

"You an expert on dreams now?" she asked, the sarcasm barely hidden.

"No, Danielle, I'm not a dream expert. I was just telling you that they are different now. It's hard to explain."

She coughed and then snuffed her cigarette out in the ashtray. "Well, I gotta get dressed. I have a full day today."

"Danielle, are you happy?"

She brushed back her hair. "Where's this going, Jim? What do you need me to say?" She sighed, "I really do have to get going."

He shook his head, looking back at his cereal bowl. "No, I'm fine. I was just going to, ah, talk to you about something. I can talk to you later."

"Tell you what, when I get home tonight, we'll talk. I really have to get moving." She walked out of the kitchen towards the bedroom. "Don't forget to put the milk away," she shouted, closing the bedroom door.

He shook his head, remembering a time when she would never take her morning shower without him. It had been a time of wonderful intimacy, a chance to start the day off right. A distant low rumble of thunder rolled across his backyard announcing another day of cold drizzle. Depressed by the weather and further evidence that the romance was truly over, he set the cereal bowl on the floor for the dogs, trying to think of a reason not to get in his truck and drive until his wheels hit ocean water.

Through all the self-pity, he knew in his heart that she still loved him, needed him on some obscure level, and maybe if he put in the effort, she would start responding to him like he needed her to. The idea of that possible renewal sustained him. Its promise gave him what little hope he had left.

He cleared the rest of the breakfast dishes from the table as a heavy rain started to fall. Just before heading into the bedroom to get dressed, he heard his cell phone on the kitchen counter buzz. He checked the clock above the stove, surprised that anyone would make a call at seven-thirty in the morning. The phone continued to buzz as he picked it up and checked the number. 7777777, weird number, he thought, answering, "Hello?"

"Hi, Jim, how are you this morning?" replied the voice, a voice strangely familiar.

"I'm fine, who is this?"

"That's a complicated question, Jim. You see, I'm many things to many people."

"Listen, pal, I'm not buying real estate or gold or anything else you're selling, so put me on your do-not-call-list right away. You got that?"

"Jim, I'm not selling anything. I just wanted..."

He snapped the phone shut to stop the conversation. The last thing he needed was a pushy telemarketer. He tossed the phone on the counter and was suddenly startled when the voice continued. "Now, Jim, that wasn't very nice. A little courtesy goes a long way in this world. You really need to work on that."

Cross slowly stepped up to the phone as if it had turned into a deadly snake. "How the hell are you still there? The phone is off. How can you still be connected?"

"Settle down, Jim. We'll talk again soon. You have yourself a nice morning."

He picked up the phone. "Who is this?" he shouted.

"Jim, who are you talking to?"

Startled, he spun around to see Danielle standing beside the refrigerator buttoning her blouse. "Your phone is off, honey."

Confused, he looked at his phone and then at her. "No, this guy called, a telemarketer. I hung up on him. But then he was able to stay connected somehow and kept talking."

She smiled without humor as she flipped her hair over her collar. "Okay, whatever you say. If you don't mind, I need my blazer picked up at the dry cleaners today. Would you mind getting it?" She dropped a crumpled ten-dollar bill on the counter. "That should cover it," she said as she hurried to the back part of the house to finish getting ready for work.

"Sucks when she does that," announced the voice in the phone. As if he had been hit by an electrical shock, Cross dropped the phone on the kitchen table. "Jesus Christ!" he shouted staring at the device. "Danielle, come here, quick!"

"It's okay, Jim. You're the one I need to talk to, not the lovely Danielle."

He snatched the phone off the table. "All right, you son-of-a-bitch, how do you know my wife's name?"

"C'mon, Jim. Keep up. You just called her name," replied the voice, laughing.

"You tell me how you're able to stay connected on this phone!" he shouted.

"Honey, are you okay?" He turned and saw Danielle looking at him intently.

"It's the phone. The guy is still on the phone. Here.." he said, handing it to her.

Rolling her eyes, she took the phone and held it to her ear. "Nothing but a dial tone, Jim," she replied, handing it back. "Look, I really don't have time right now. I'm already late." She picked up her purse and car keys and headed for the front door. "I will call you later," she announced. "Go take a nap or something. Maybe you'll feel better." She opened the door and left, leaving the faint smell of her familiar perfume hanging lightly in the air.

"Hey, Jim, you there?" The voice from the phone made him jump.

"Listen, pal, if I ever find out how you're doing this, I'm going to…"

"Hey, no threats there, tough guy," interrupted the voice. "Let's try and keep this civil, okay?"

"Civil! You want me to be civil after you hacked my phone? If I find out who you are and where you're at, I'll show you how civil I can be, you son-of-a-bitch."

"Ah, c'mon, Jim. Let's try and keep the profanity down to a minimum, okay?"

Cross ripped the back off the phone and pulled out the battery, tossing it on the kitchen table.

"Now, Jim, did you think that was really going to stop our conversation?" the voice continued. Stunned, Cross threw the receiver across the room, shattering it against the wall. He stood still in the middle of the room, fully expecting the voice to return. He waited. Several minutes passed, and he walked over to pick up the broken phone.

"Ah, Jim, you feel better now?" questioned the same, irritatingly calm voice.

Cross stood trembling with a mixture of fear and rage while looking at the broken phone. "What do you want? How is this possible?"

"Tell you what, Jim, maybe we should meet face to face, you know, to get to know each other. I think that might help the situation."

"There's no situation. When I see you I'm going to take your head off!"

The voice laughed. "Really? You know that would be quite a feat on your part."

"Yeah, why's that?"

"Well, to began with, Jim, I am not a half-drunk drug dealer who's trying to rip you off in an alley somewhere."

Cross instantly felt weak in the knees. "What, what did you just say?" he said, almost in a whisper.

The voice chuckled, "There is nothing hidden, Jim. Haven't you ever read the Bible? I know all about your altercation last week. Pretty traumatic, huh?"

His head was spinning. "Who, I mean, what's this about? What's going on?" Cross said tersely.

There was a long pause. "Jim, calm down. What I need you to do is go get in your truck and head over to the Denny's on Fourth Street. I'll meet you there in about ten minutes."

"Listen," he shouted at the phone. "Who is this? What do you want?"

There was no reply.

If Cross had been able to see with the eyes of true perception, he would have seen the shape behind the voice. The Messenger stood, in his own reality, less then three feet away. He smiled watching Cross stomp the remnants of the phone to bits. He laughed as he saw his new project grab the pistol off the counter and then head quickly out the door. "Ah, Mister Cross," he thought, "you have such a long long way to go. It's sad that so much time is wasted on negative emotions before the real education begins." Sad indeed.

***

Kitchens picked up the phone on the second ring. He had just finished eating lunch at his desk again, an endeavor that had branded him as being tight by the other homicide Dicks on the floor. He preferred to think of himself as thrifty. Besides, every dime saved was a dime he would need for retirement. "Kitchens."

"Yeah, this is Cronehaur over at the ME 's office."

"Go ahead, Doc. What do you got?" It had been four days since he and the ME had bagged the bodies in the alley. Hopefully forensics had turned something up.

Cronehaur coughed heavily before answering, "Well, both your victims died from high caliber slugs to the head. My guess would be a forty-five. Both had pronounced levels of alcohol and stimulants in their blood, pretty standard chemical courage."

Kitchens sat back in his chair. "Anything else, Doc? Anything unusual?"

"Well, I may have something. The victim on the ground had paint in the wounds."

"Paint, what kind of paint?"

"It's blue, dark blue. Ran some tests and it's car paint. Waiting to get something back from the Feds on what kind of car it might have been from. My guess is that whoever capped this guy did so by shooting through the door. The wound channel on his neck and head seems to back that up .You know what that means don't ya?"

"Sure do, Doc. It means I'm looking for a blue car or truck that has bullet holes in it."

The ME coughed again over the phone. "That's right. Anyway, that's all I have right now. If I get more, I'll give you a call. I gotta go have a cigarette."

"All right, Doc. Thanks for the information. I'll come by later and pick up your report."

"That's fine."

He hung up the phone encouraged that he at least had a bit more information about the shooter than he had before. He knew that his chances of finding the bad guy hinged on a lot of hard work, long hours, and a bit of luck. About a third of the homicides he had worked on were still pending an arrest and conviction. They were mostly gang related with no witness or anyone with a sense of civic duty coming forward with a statement.

No, something about this one was not normal as these things go. There were no predictable dots to connect. Whoever this shooter was appeared to be cool under fire, maybe possessing a skill-set that made this kind of encounter manageable. Chasing down someone who could kill with precision, with this kind of firepower was always an unnerving proposition. Many a detective had lost his life or become severely injured going after this kind of suspect. The only thing that kept these assailants from winning the game was the fact that the guys in blue had more players, more guns, more bullets, and more time. He would be careful on this one, really careful.

Chapter Three

By eight that morning, Cross was just pulling into the Denny's west-side parking lot, not having any idea what the guy looked like that he was supposed to meet. He had thought seriously of not showing up but chalking up the whole weird experience to a really sophisticated hacker who was not worth his time. Yet the guy seemed to know about the shooting and that was something that needed exploring. He pulled his truck into one of the far stalls and turned off the engine, trying to think of what to do next.

He watched as an elderly couple slowly moved across the lot and then disappeared into the restaurant. Minutes later, a heavyset woman came out of the building and got into a car parked in one of the handicap spots. "This is dumb," he mumbled out loud. Just before starting his truck to leave, a sudden heavy knock on the passenger side window made him jump. A large man with a heavy dark beard and sunglasses stood smiling on the other side of the glass. "Hi, Jim," he announced, pointing to the locked door. "Open up. Let's talk."

Cross hit the unlock button on the armrest with his left hand while drawing the pistol with his right. As the man opened the door, he raised the weapon. "Get in, you son-of-a-bitch, or I'm going to drop you right here."

The man smiled as he got into the truck. "C'mon, Jim, you don't really mean that." In a microsecond he had reached up and snatched the weapon from Cross's hand, so fast and forcefully that Cross was rendered speechless. The man smiled as he bent the gun in half as if it had been made of dough. "Here, you can put this away now. Although I doubt it's going to fit in your holster anymore."

In numb astonishment, Cross slowly took the bent pistol. Torn between crying and laughing, he nearly inaudibly replied, "I, ah, what the hell?"

"It's okay, Jim. Just relax. I'm sure I have your attention now." The man looked at him smiling. "Am I correct, Jim? Do I have your attention?"

Cross still could not believe what he had just seen. Nobody could bend a steel handgun in half like that.

"How did you do that?" he asked, already considering how he was going to get out of the truck.

The man sat back in his seat and ran his fingers through his thick black hair with a sigh. "Okay, Jim, here's how we are going to proceed. I'm here as a guide, a coach, as it were. A lot of what I am saying will not make any sense to you right now, but it will in time."

Cross quickly flipped the door handle in an attempt to flee the cab. He was able to get one foot on the pavement right before a mind numbing pain of searing intensity jolted through his hip and right thigh. Frozen in trembling agony, he sat half in and half out of the cab, grunting and gritting his teeth from the growing pain. As he gripped the steering wheel with white knuckles, a new level of pain coursed through his body. Never in his life of sixty years had he ever felt anything even close to this gut wrenching agony. Just before he was about to pass out, the pain suddenly stopped. Breathless he slumped over the steering wheel, sweat running down his back to his waist. "I can't breathe," he gasped, trying to stay upright.

"Oh, you can breathe, Jim. Now do I have your attention?"

Cross nodded with his head resting on the steering wheel. "Yeah, yeah, you have my attention," he replied, slowly getting back into his seat and closing the door. The pain had left him weak and disoriented. "What happened? What was that?" he asked, catching his breath.

The Messenger was now looking at him closely. "That was a correction, Jim, a mild bit of discipline that you sorely needed. Hopefully, we don't have to do that again. I draw no pleasure from seeing you suffer."

Cross wiped the sweat from his forehead. "Who or what are you, pal? Am I dreaming this?"

The man laughed, "Well that's complicated, Jim. Let's table that question for some other time. Right now I just need you to understand that I am in your life now and that you are going to be going through a bit of self discovery."

"Why me?"

"Ah, another good question. But, one I fear will not be answered by someone in my position."

Cross shook his head. "I don't understand any of this. What's your position? Who the hell are you anyway?"

The man leaned in close. "I'm a servant, Jim." He snapped his fingers and smiled. "Someone who does what he is told."

"I can't believe this is happening," replied Cross. "What am I supposed to do?"

The man chuckled as he opened his door. "Tell you what, Jim. Why don't you go inside and get yourself something cool to drink. Maybe get a hamburger or something. It'll make you feel better. I hear the food is pretty good here."

"You brought me here for this?" he shouted as the man closed the door.

The Messenger turned around and smiled. "I'll be in touch, Jim."

"Hey, you owe me twelve-hundred bucks for my pistol, you son-of-a-bitch!" he shouted as he watched the man walk away and then disappear behind a semi parked at the far end of the lot.

Cross had no idea how long he sat in his truck that afternoon trying to get his head around what had just happened to him. Minutes of introspection turned into hours until the orange-red halogen lights of the parking lot illuminated the inside of his truck letting him know the sun had gone down.

Before finally starting his truck, he took another look at the pistol lying on the seat next to him - bent double. A chill ran up his spine at the thought that someone or some thing had actually been able to do that. But more unnerving - whatever was going to happen to him would be controlled by this Messenger, something that took human form but was definitely not human.

As if all of this hadn't been enough to handle, Jim had no idea how he was going to explain this to Danielle. Driving home through the early evening Detroit traffic, he let his body relax, resigned to the fact that he was not in control. Nothing he had to say about the day would make any sense to Danielle. Hell, nothing made sense to him anymore. Nothing.

***

The shattered plastic pieces of phone were the first things she saw that evening when she returned home from her shift at the hospital. Danielle had enjoyed her job in the ICU over the last seven years. Her career as an RN was on the fast track. In fact, rumor had it that she was in the running for director of the unit, probably within the next year. Not bad for the daughter of a hardware salesman out of Sedalia, Kansas.

Her mother, a life-long smoker, had died when she was in her junior year of high school, a year that for most girls held the promise of dances, first loves, and college plans. For years she had held a hard-edged anger against her mother for dying so young. She had watched her slowly shrink from a robust forty-one-year-old active woman who loved dancing and family gatherings, to an air-starved ghost of a person. The cancer and struggle had been so destructive to her body that at the time of her death she had been buried in a child's coffin.

As funerals go, it had been one of those intensely melancholy affairs that followed an agonizing death that left two teenage daughters and an adoring husband in crushing grief. Yet the only visual image she carried from that oddly warm March afternoon was a smudge of red clay dirt left on the front right side of her mother's light blue coffin left behind as it had been placed on the lowering rack by the pallbearers. Throughout the ceremony she had stared at that smudge as she had tuned out every other sight and sound around her. Even at the age of sixteen, she had been acutely aware of the enormity of her loss. The mother-daughter connection would never have the chance to blossom. She would miss having her mom there for homecoming, for graduation, for college moving day and every other meaningful life transition. All had been lost on the acrid wisps of cigarette smoke, and she hated her for it.

For years the anger and resentment had fuelled a nearly pathological drive towards her studies. She had graduated high school with a 4.0 propelling her into a top-notch nursing program where she graduated first in her class. She had moved throughout the nursing field from ER trauma nurse where she saw all the suicide attempts and drug overdoses she could ever care to see, to OBGYN, before finally landing in the spot that suited her best - the intensive care unit. She thrived in the ICU environment of absolutes, concrete measurable progress toward health, or the equally measurable spiral into death.

The steady procession of broken bodies moved in and out of her ward in cold clinical regularity. Car accident victims, gunshot survivors, injuries from barroom brawls to motorcycle and skydiving accidents all rolled across the polished and sterile white floors of her ward, never knowing the heart of the plain, yet oddly attractive, brown-eyed nurse.

Ten years ago she had married Jim when he was hip-deep in his career as a security consultant. His work took him frequently overseas to Iraq, Afghanistan, Africa, South America, and any other war-torn, war-weary part of the world where there were opportunities for men of his skill set. He had been living in hotels and airplanes, and it had given them precious little time together. But two years ago, when he turned sixty, the phone calls for work in his field stopped coming. She had watched as the man she loved went from a strong, self-confident provider to a frightened, moody, overly cautious, distant, and angry man.

The savings had all but dried up along with any hope of employment that could come close to providing the kind of money he had been making. The situation had left them totally dependent on her nurse's salary. Despite her objections, Jim had decided to grow medical marijuana. Even though she was fearful of this new venture, nervous about how it would affect their home, she was happy to see him excited about something, an excitement she hadn't seen for several years. He had used the last of the money set aside to order seed, chemicals and other equipment to get his small business off the ground. He seemed to be keeping his head down, keeping a low profile, and she was becoming a little more comfortable with his plan.

Little did she know that his latest "venture" had pushed him to kill. Nor did she have any idea that something was about to change their lives forever.

***

As he drove into the driveway he saw Danielle's car. A chill of anxiety and fear rolled through his body as he sat in his truck trying to figure out how he was going to explain this whole weird mess. He stepped out of his truck and headed into the house, knowing one way or another this was it.

Danielle was in the kitchen pouring herself a much-needed glass of red wine. "So how was your day?" she asked, taking a long drink.

He laid the bent pistol on the counter, not knowing any other way to start the conversation. "Ah, it's been a little weird."

She slowly set her glass down staring at the gun as if it had grown legs and was about to run off the counter. "What, how, what happened? Is THAT the new one you bought?"

He sat down heavily on one of the counter stools, more tired than he had been in years. "Yes, that's the new one I just bought. Is that what you're worried about, the money I spent? Jesus, Danielle, I show you a gun that's bent into a pretzel. Don't you want to know how it got that way?"

She shook her head, open-mouthed. "Ah, yeah, Jim, that was going to be my next question. What the hell is wrong with you? I just got home. You were acting crazy this morning and now you show me this? Why don't you cut me some god-dammed slack, okay?" she shouted, trembling.

He shook his head, smiling, realizing that she was right. He was pushing her way too hard. He had had all day to think about this. "Sorry, Sweetheart, I, ah, I've had a really strange day. Hell, it's been a strange week. I'm sorry."

She took another long drink, calming a bit. "Okay, since we are now talking, tell me about the gun. And while you're at it, tell me about the two bullet holes and the ruined headrest in my car. Did you think I wouldn't notice?"

"You saw the holes?"

"Jim, are you insane? Of course I saw the holes the day after you borrowed the car last week. I have been waiting for an explanation since. I finally took the car down to Rhymes Garage and the holes have been pounded down and filled in. They also ordered me a new headrest. So, now, are you going to tell me what happened? I'm sure it won't be the same thing I told Jeff down at the garage."

"So, what did you tell him?"

"I made up this story about you shooting the gun by accident."

He shook his head. "How would I have done that, Danielle? I'm a weapons expert. You make me look like an idiot."

She nodded to the bent pistol. "Well, that certainly is impressive. Can't wait to hear how that happened."

"You know, sarcasm on your part is not helping me here."

She let out a snorting laugh, "Jim, are you kidding me? At this point I would welcome anything that would help explain all this. You've gone from a highly respected international security consultant to a senior citizen marijuana grower who shoots holes in my car and walks around with a brand new gun that's bent in two. Oh, and to top it off, you apparently destroyed your phone, which is still not paid for by the way. All because you think somebody is calling you even when it's off, I assume? Honestly, Jim, a little sarcasm and a lot more wine are pretty much called for right now."

He thought for a moment as she stood staring at him with that same look she had given him when he told her that he wanted to get back into skydiving last year. "Okay, I see your point. When you put it all together like that, things do sound out of whack."

Her look softened into one of tired resignation. "Jim, just tell me the truth. I can handle that. No more lies, please."

"Well, okay," he began slowly. "I met an angel, at least I think he's an angel - still not sure. He's the one that bent my gun."

A single tear rolled down her cheek. "You son-of-a-bitch," she whispered. "You're not going to tell me, are you? You're really not going to keep this real between us." She tossed the glass into the sink, shattering it. "I'm done. When you really want to talk, let me know," she shouted walking down the hallway, slamming the bedroom door behind her.

He sat, looking at his pistol, knowing full well that no matter what he had said her reaction would have been the same. He had killed two men with that gun and hadn't thought much about the whole affair since it had happened. Had he slid that far? Had he dropped off the emotional scale of normal human compassion to the point that nothing mattered other than just getting through the next hour, the next minute, the next second of the day? Without an answer, he picked up his bent pistol and headed to the basement to check on his plants.

He was proud of his grow boxes. They put growing medical-grade marijuana into an almost factory like precision with the water regulated, the light regulated and the process formulated for high-grade Cannabis.

It was almost too easy. It was a virtual "plug it in and forget it operation" that was producing far more crop than one person could ever use for personal needs. Every eight to nine weeks he was processing a pound of thirty-percent THC grade-A bud, worth at least five to six thousands dollars on the black market.

He knew the more grow boxes he invested in, the more product he could harvest. Money, or the lack of it, was no longer going to be an issue. Danielle had no idea how well he was starting to do financially. It was a shame. He wanted to talk to her about it because if she knew how much money was now coming in from his weed sales she wouldn't have to work anymore. "After all, wasn't that the very reason he started all this?" he thought, checking the PH level in one of the boxes. "Hell, all of this had been for her."

Sadly, he realized that because all they did now was yell at each other and slam doors, he wasn't able to share with her the satisfaction of having achieved this level of success. He longed to see her relax in that knowledge. Upstairs, above him, he could hear her thumping around in the bedroom, her footfalls quick, purposeful, and angry.

***

Later that night, as he lay trying to sleep in the guest room, a strange sensation began to course through his body. It was unlike anything he had ever experienced. It was not pain, but an awareness of discomfort as if he was sleeping on the ground and had a rock under his back.

He turned the nightstand lamp on just as the muscles in his neck began to slowly cramp. For a fleeting moment he thought he was having a heart attack. He checked the idea of calling out to Danielle. She would probably think he was being melodramatic, trying to gain some sympathy after the argument they had had earlier that evening.

A sudden heavy sweat washed over him, nearly taking his breath away. "What the hell?" he whispered, lying back. Disjointed voices, shouting, screaming and crying came out of the darkness. Just before passing out, the heavy, musty smell of fresh mud and gun-smoke filled his consciousness.

He fought for breath like a man drowning in freezing water, as the cacophony of sound and smells hovered over him in the dark. The vision pressed him flat, its emotional weight pinning him down as tears of fear rolled down the side of his face and into his ears while he fought to stay aware, willing himself not to fall into the void of nothingness. Just as the last bit of his strength and resolve faded, the attack stopped as quickly as it had come. His vision cleared, the pain was gone, leaving him totally exhausted. The only sounds now - the gentle ticking of the alarm clock and Danielle's slow rhythmic breathing in the next room.

Nearly paralyzed by fatigue, he closed his eyes and drifted off to sleep where the strangeness of the event lingered in his sub consciousness. He became aware that he had oddly recognized the dialect and tone of the voices even though they had been speaking French, a language he neither spoke nor understood.

Questions drifted with him through his dreams as the hours passed. Fate already had the answer.

Outside in the moonlight, where truth and lies can blend and twist together, the hidden boundary of his reality had been breached. Thoughts, fears, and actions combined creating it's own energy - it's own power. On the emotional battleground, there would be no quarter, no mercy.

James would soon have to absorb and adjust to the new truth of who and what he was. Death, his death, with all its terrible and absolute assuredness, was getting closer. Even in sleep, he could sense it moving around in the moonlight. He rolled tighter into his covers, confident of his utter helplessness. In his dreams the light of a thousand stars blew out. Things were about to change.

Chapter Four

It was ten-thirty the next morning and Kitchens was just leaving the scene of another homicide. A body of a well-known drug dealer from his old neighborhood had been found in the backyard of an abandoned house up on West Third Street, one of the most dangerous blocks in Detroit. As usual, no one had heard or seen anything - standard operating procedure for this part of town. Third murder this month on the block and nobody was talking to the Heat.

Urban decay was a term that the politicians used as a blanket statement for everything bad coming off the street, a pretense that local government gave for having given up on making it better. Urban renewal, shovel-ready projects, infrastructure investment had been the jargon of the well-heeled and insulated. But to Kitchens, they were all nothing more than social tourists with no real understanding of how to fix what was happening on the south side nor the patience to listen to those that did.

The city was dying and everyone who had stayed knew it. The increasing body-count kept up a steady pace, predator and prey changing roles, sometimes within hours. As he drove through his old neighborhood, he knew that his time behind the badge was getting short. Now, there were second and third generation victims within the same family, the vicious cycle of grinding poverty, drugs, and the hope of fast money taking them out quickly. Turning west onto Jackson Avenue, he spotted one of his unofficial informants leaning against the pole of a stop sign.

Kitchen put down the passenger side window as he rolled up. "Yo, William, watcha doin man?"

William Jefferson Tamro was a fixture in the neighborhood. The young gangsters who ran the block had written him off as an old drunk years ago, and it was that status, having nothing of value to take or to add, that had kept him alive all these years. He kept to himself most of the time, living off his disability check and whatever cans and bottles he could find during the week.

Willie Jay, as he was known, kept his head down and his eyes open. To the casual observer he was just another old shabbily dressed black man, pushing a trash bag laden shopping cart with one bad wheel. To Kitchens he was the eyes and ears of the neighborhood and a solid conduit for street level information. If it went down in the neighborhood, Willie knew about it. Even from a distance of six feet, Kitchens could smell the alcohol on Willie's breath, the smell of the cheap wine blended with the smell of old sweat and dirt as he leaned into the passenger side window.

"Detective Kitchen, I thought that was you rolling up. What you doin down here?"

"Ah you know, brother, trying to keep the peace. You doin all right?"

Willie chuckled. "Been okay. Still trying to get paid, you know."

Kitchen reached over and handed him a ten-dollar bill. "Here you go, man. Go get yourself something to eat. Go on, take it now."

William took the bill and quickly stuffed it into his pocket. "Thank you, sir. You're a good man."

"Naw, Willie you'd do the same for me. Say, you see anything I need to know about? I got a lot of people getting shot and not a whole lot of information as to why."

Willie smiled. "Ah, you know how it is. People got something other people want. Old story, nothing new."

"Yeah, I know, but I have to do my job and try to stop it. This is my old neighborhood, you know. I've gotta do what I can."

Willie thought for a moment. "You ever find that white man?" he asked, lighting a cigarette.

"White man, what white man?"

Willie took a long drag and then blew the smoke outside the window. Kitchen could see that WJ was trying to think of a way to say something. "What you got, man? C'mon now. You know something. You gotta help me out. This is serious."

Willie J flicked his cigarette into the gutter and then leaned back in through the window. "The word is that a white man killed Kojack and Holloway."

Kitchen was surprised by how matter-of-fact Willie had made the statement. "What's a white man doing down in the projects?"

"Folks say he was moving chronic. Said it was powerful shit."

Kitchen thought for a moment. "You got a description? A car? Anything?"

Willie J stepped back from the window as several young black teens walked by.

"Five-O," announced one of the kids just loud enough to be heard. The other three laughed and kept walking. Willie J nodded in their direction. "Young and dumb," he said, watching the youths cross the street.

"Willie, what's all this about a white man. Tell me some more. I got things to do."

Willie leaned back into the window still watching the youths as they walked away. "That Carson punk and his brother are always talking shit."

"Willie, forget them. Tell me about the white guy. C'mon now."

Willie J turned his head, spit on the ground and leaned back in the window. "Two days before Holloway got shot, I seen him riding around with a white guy. Never seen him around here before."

Kitchen quickly started writing on a small pad. "What color was the car?"

Willie thought for a moment. "Blue, a blue two-door."

Kitchen stopped writing, remembering what the ME had said about the blue paint found in Kojack's wounds. "Would you be able to recognize this man again if you saw a picture?"

Willie laughed. "Hell, you know all those white boys look alike... Maybe."

Kitchen handed him one of his cards. "Take my card, Willie J. You see this white guy around here again, you call me. You hear?"

"You know I don't have no phone."

"Willie, you see this man, you find a goddamn phone and let me know. Now, it's important. We don't want anyone else getting killed out here. All right? I'm serious, Willie. You call me."

Willie J backed away from the car, smiling. "Okay, All right, I'll call."

Kitchen put his car back in gear as another car drove up behind him and honked. "Remember what I said, Willie," shouted Kitchen, slowly driving away.

The older man gave a half-wave as he turned toward his heavily stacked shopping cart. He shook his head, knowing full well he would never call the detective or any other police officer concerning the shooting.

As far as he was concerned, he had said enough. It was a bad deal that Deon Carson and his shithead brother had seen him talking to the cops. There was no telling what that would lead to. Just getting through the day in the hood was tough enough when you were old and slow. And since his hearing had gone bad, he had had a hard time knowing when the punks were walking up behind waiting to kick over his cart. He was the neighborhood joke, the funny old man with no teeth and dirty clothes. Except when they took his cans or broke the bottles he had found, he was invisible to them. Well, things were about to change.

As he slowly began to push his buggy, he chuckled at an idea he had. He was going to handle those Carson brothers. With the coin he would get off the last of his cans and bottles and the ten dollars Kitchen had just given him, he would finally have enough money to get his pistol out of the pawnshop. The only thing he had left of his family was his dad's small 38. He was seventy-seven years old with nothing left to live for except for this one more thing, one more chance to feel some control over his life.

Tomorrow night he would walk in, just as cool as a summer breeze, buy a cold beer down at Diamond's Bar and Grill where all the bone thugs and the Carson brothers played dominos. "Yeah, ol' Willie J be taking care of business tomorrow," he thought, smiling. He would drink his beer and then shoot both those boys in the head, his tormenters, the ones that had pushed him around and made fun of him for years. He'd show em. The punks who had knocked over his cart and stole his cans would be dead before they hit the floor. He'd show 'em all. "Yeah, gonna be a good day," he thought. "Pay back was a cold bitch. Goddamn right."

***

The early morning sun filled the room with a brightness that slowly pulled him out of sleep. He thought he had heard Danielle leave earlier but wasn't sure if he had dreamed the noise. "Danielle!" he shouted, still groggy. "You home?"

There was no response. He slowly sat up and put his feet on the floor, trying to understand the dreams and the feelings that lingered after them. He could not put his finger on it, but he knew something had changed. Something had been set in motion. He got up, brushed his teeth, and shaved like he always did, following the habits of someone who had to be somewhere, someone who had a job, someone of respectability and purpose.

Fully dressed, he headed downstairs and saw that Danielle had left her dirty breakfast dishes in the sink for him to clean up again. He poured his coffee and was about to sit down at the kitchen counter when he heard a voice behind him, making him drop his cup to the floor.

"Morning, Jim."

"Shit!" he shouted, spinning around angrily.

The Messenger stood in the middle of the living room.

"How the hell did you get in my house?" shouted Cross kicking the bar stool out of the way.

"Hey, Jim, sorry to startle you. Settle down."

Cross quickly pulled a large butcher knife from the block next to the sink. "You got thirty seconds to get out of my house, you son-of-a – bitch, or I'm gonna cut you from asshole to elbow."

The Messenger smiled. "Well, I think we are way past that kind of action, Jim. Now, put the knife down before you hurt yourself."

Cross took a step closer, the knife held out in front of him. "You heard what I said."

The Messenger sighed. "Are you really going to push this, Jim? What do I need to do to convince you that I am in control of your situation?"

Cross thought for a moment. "Who the hell are you anyway, or, should I say, what are you?"

Faster than he could blink, the Messenger was suddenly inches from Cross's face. Cross felt as if his hand was being slowly torn off the end of his arm, a crushing, vice-like grip firmly planted around his hand.

"Jim," whispered the Messenger, "I am someone whose time you do not want to waste."

The Messenger stared deep into Cross's eyes. "Do we understand each other, Jim?" he asked calmly.

"Ahhgh, my hand, you're breaking it."

"Jim, do we have an understanding yet? I really don't have time for this."

"Okay, okay, just stop crushing my hand! Geez!" Cross squirmed with the throbbing pain.

The Messenger dropped his grip and stepped back slowly. "Okay, let's try and be civil, all right?" he said, smiling.

Cross collapsed to the floor, landing on his knees. "Feels like you broke every bone," he moaned, cradling his hand. He slowly rose to his feet and fell back onto the couch, trying to catch his breath. "Go on!" he shouted angrily. "Finish it. I can't fight you. Go ahead and kill me."

The Messenger sat down on the coffee table across from him, staring intently. "Is that what you think I'm here for, to kill you?"

"Isn't it?" questioned Cross, confused by the Messenger's demeanor. "I mean, what else is going on here?"

The Messenger thought for a moment as a slight smile crossed his face. "No, Jim, you are actually being given a great gift, and I am here to deliver it."

"I don't understand. Are you some kind of angel, some kind of spirit?"

The Messenger laughed. "We're all spirits, Jim." He stood up and walked to the refrigerator. "You have any orange juice, Jim? I really like orange juice."

Cross slowly got to his feet, his head spinning with questions. "Hey, look, you have to give me something here, okay? I mean, I think I'm about to lose it; this is so over-the-top surreal. Just who the hell are you? Why does this involve me?"

The Messenger closed the refrigerator door. "Well I guess this is as good a time as any to start the transition.

"What do you mean 'transition'? What's going to happen?"

The Messenger looked at him intently. "Something incredible, my friend. You get to be a witness to the human condition. It will be a magnificent revelation."

"Hey, listen, I just want to live out the rest of my own life, okay?"

The Messenger stepped up close. "I understand your trepidation. But it's really out of my hands. I'm just a messenger. You're actually very lucky to even see me. Most people in your situation don't see me till after the transition."

Cross backed up as the Messenger stepped closer. He could feel the panic start to rise. "Hey listen, just stay away from me."

The Messenger slowly raised his arms as a golden bright light filled the room. "It's time," he said softly.

Cross stepped back, squinting at the growing brightness. The sound of a roaring wind filled his ears as the light, now all around him, became blinding, as if he were looking into the sun. A sudden, searing bolt of pain shot through the left side of his head, driving him to the floor in agony. Cross became aware of the Messenger kneeling over him, speaking in soft tones in a language he had never heard before just as things went completely dark. The pain vanished as suddenly as it had hit, leaving him in a state of exhausted bliss.

He let the Messenger's words soothe his spirit as he drifted into the growing darkness with a peace like nothing he had ever experienced. All the pretense, all the lies of his life fell away like diseased scales, exposing the clean healthy skin of who he really was. He floated in a dark, cool fog of total acceptance, total understanding, letting the heavy, ethereal wind driven by the Messenger's words move him deeper into the cloud.

The momentum of the passage increased, memories and faces of friends and family flashing by, telling long forgotten stories of pain and triumph.

He knew what this was, yet this realization of death carried no fear. The Messenger's words continued as the images of his life rushed by. All the wrongs, all the hurt he had caused in other people's lives manifested in an odd background of colors behind the images.

Raw emotion manifested as hues of color either as bright, brilliant, dazzling splashes of light, or as darkened tinges of black or dusty brown-like old photographs left out in the sun. Suddenly suspended by an unseen force above a great chasm, its depth infinite, the train of images slowed and then stopped.

He gently drifted in midair, still without fear, intuitively knowing that he was where he was supposed to be. He suddenly realized that the words that had carried him into the darkness had stopped and he felt, for the first time, a rush of fear of falling. He rolled onto his back in the darkness with arms outstretched feeling the increasing rush and power of a wind roar by. He cried out in terror, helpless in the fall, as his speed continued to increase. He dropped downward, as if into a bottomless well, the cool, comfortable temperature becoming an uncomfortable warmth. Smells of damp earth and rocks filled his senses as he seemed to drop endlessly. The disjointed voices of men, shouting in fear, echoed in the darkness.

Suddenly, with a mind-numbing jolt, he slammed to a stop. The air blasted out of his lungs with a tremendous force, leaving him gasping and grunting for breath.

As his vision began to clear he was stunned to see that he was lying in a shallow, muddy ditch. It was raining, the cold, pounding downpour, sending shivers down his back.

He rolled onto his side as he tried to focus on his surroundings. The sound of muted thunder rolled across the landscape and he blinked the rain out of his eyes to see muddy ground all around him choked with strands of twisted barbwire and broken fence posts.

More thunder thumped through the air as a voice, suddenly beside him shouted above the rain. "Get your ass up, Marine! We gotta get to the wood line. Move! Move! Move!"

Stunned beyond words, Cross looked over his shoulder at the mud and sweat stained face of a soldier wearing a filthy brown uniform and a World War I doughboy helmet.

"What, What, is going on?" he stammered, as the soldier roughly pulled him to his feet. He was shoved out of the ditch as the man rushed past him in the direction of the woods some distance away.

As if on wooden legs, he stumbled through the mud after the man, suddenly aware of the fact that he was running within a group of soldiers. One of the men thrust a mud-encrusted pump shot gun into his hands. "You dropped this!" he shouted, running past as a thunderclap explosion from above flattened the group into the mud.

Screams of pain filled the air as shrapnel from the air burst shell hit flesh. Cross fell into a shallow, muddy, water-filled hole next to a soldier wearing sergeant stripes.

"Jesus Christ!" he shouted as a second shell burst high overhead. "What's going on? Where am I?"

The soldier shot him a quick confused glance. "Some place called Bella Wood, France, you dumb shit. Better pull yourself together!" he shouted as a third and then fourth shell thundered overhead. "Welcome to the goddamned war."

Chapter Five

"So, you found him on the floor when you got home from work, around five-thirty?"

"I, ah, yeah, it was about that time," she replied with a sigh. "He was lying on the living room floor. I checked his pulse, saw that he had a blown pupil, and called 911."

The doctor checked the MRI pictures again, looking through the bottom of his glasses. "Well, it's a pretty severe bleed. He's stable but I'm afraid that the damage is fairly extensive, Danielle."

She brushed back a tear, "Is he going to die?"

The doctor set his glasses on the desk. "Danielle, I always try to give the family members of any stroke victim the most honest assessment that I can. Jim has suffered a severe CVA and is in critical condition. To be brutally honest I am surprised that he has held on this long."

Danielle wiped away more tears. "So you're saying he's not going to make it?"

"I'm saying that his condition is critical. But there is always hope."

She stood up, not knowing what else to do and walked over to the office window, watching a light early rain patter against the window. For a second she tried to remember if she had rolled the windows up on her car and then began to consider if she had locked the front door of the house before she had left to follow the ambulance to the hospital.

She winced at the memory of seeing the broken coffee cup on the floor of the kitchen and Jim's body, nearly lifeless and pale crumpled near the couch. He must have been lying there all day. It was amazing he had survived.

"So what can we do now?" she asked, already knowing what he would say.

The doctor shook his head. "Nothing more can be done right now. He's stable and that's about as much as we can hope for."

She had heard the phrases before, been in the room with strangers in her role as a nurse, had stood in the corner and watched the pieces of other people's lives fall apart as the new reality set in. Things would never be the same in their lives, just as they would never be the same in hers.

The surreal feel of the moment took her out of herself, leaving a disconcerting detachment like she had never experienced before. The doctor handed her a small stack of papers.

"Danielle, you're going to need to sign these forms - insurance paperwork, DNR request and some long-term care options. There are also some very good hospice facilities near by."

Emotionally numb, she took the forms, suddenly feeling the room get smaller. She needed air, needed to be outside, needed to be anywhere other than in this small, cramped office where the fear of what the future would bring hung in the air like a bad smell. "I, ah, I have to go," she announced, heading for the door.

"Danielle, let me give you the number of a counselor. I think it would help."

She stopped just before leaving the office. "No, Doctor, right now the last thing I want to do is talk. I really need some air."

Before he could answer, she stepped into the brightly lit hospital hallway, closing the door behind her. She didn't even try to hide the tears as she quickly walked away.

***

"Are you going to eat that?"

Cross looked up from the metal mess kit lid that contained the bacon fat and vegetable stew he had just gotten from the chow line. "Ah, no, I'm, I'm not hungry."

The sergeant reached over and quickly dumped the stew onto his own tin. "Suit yourself. Maybe awhile till we get another hot meal. Fritz took out the mess truck last Thursday with a perfectly aimed shell." He made a whistling sound while making an arching motion, sticking his dirty finger in the stew. "Blew two cooks to pieces. Poor bastards," he smiled, shoveling spoonfuls into his mouth.

A soldier sitting next to Cross dumped the food from his tin angrily. "Serves them right. I can't eat this swill."

"Hey, Thompson," announced the sergeant, spitting small bits of food as he talked. "Don't be throwing your shit in the trench. You want to dump it out, throw it over the top."

The soldier shook his head. "Sarge, maybe you haven't noticed, but we are sitting in ankle deep mud, it's raining, and Bosworth over there just took a shit in his dug out. I don't think a tin of rancid stew is going to make any difference with what's in this trench."

The sergeant quickly continued to eat the stew on his plate, scraping out the last bit. "Waste not, want not, Thompson. Didn't your mother teach you that?" The sergeant smiled and winked at Cross. "And Bosworth!" he shouted to the men sitting further away, "you shit in your dugout again, I will personally shoot your sorry ass. You got that, Marine?"

"Yeah, Sarge," replied one of the men weakly further down the trench. Cross was having a difficult time trying to get his mind around what was happening. Evidently, he was now somewhere with the United States Marine Corps during some World War I campaign. The new sights, sounds, and smells of war were overwhelming.

Incredible as it seemed, his physical reality had shifted. His last memory was of him standing in his living room, being blinded by the light of the Messenger. Now he was sitting in a mud-filled trench, wearing a filthy military uniform with men he had never seen nor met before, strangely enough, men who seemed to know him very well.

Working to stay in control, he began to do a visual inventory of what he was carrying in the mud-caked canvas ammo pouches and uniform pockets. Two of the four chest pouches were full of red paper 12-gauge shotgun shells. There was a foot-long trench knife attached to his belt, a half-filled canteen, another smaller canvas bag that held a gas mask and an extra filter. To his surprise, he found a wallet in his back pocket along with a handful of assorted papers and letters.

"Looks like you got a case of fleas over there, Howard," announced the sergeant, leaning back in the trench. "Got ya squirming?"

"Ah, no, I'm just trying to see what I have," replied Cross, opening the wallet. He pulled out the ID card and read the name: *American Expeditionary Force* -Jonathon Edward Howard, *Rank*- Private, *Duties* –Rifleman, USMC. He looked at the grainy black and white picture and was stunned to recognize himself.

"You okay there, Howard? Looking kind of peaked," questioned the sergeant, lighting a hand-rolled cigarette.

Cross stuffed the wallet and papers back into his pocket, desperately trying to figure out what was going on. "Sergeant, how long have you known me?"

The soldier took a long drag from his cigarette, giving Cross a suspicious look. "What the hell is wrong with you, Howard? You've been acting strange all day."

"I, ah, I guess I'm just a bit rattled from the shelling."

The soldier laughed. "Jesus, Howard, we've been pounded for months now. You're not shell-shocked, are ya?"

Cross looked down at his mud-splattered hands trying to think of a way to verbalize what he was thinking. "I forgot your name," he said softly.

The sergeant flipped his cigarette into the mud. "Okay, that's it. Get your ass up and head over to the Doc's dugout."

A low roll of thunder rumbled across the broken landscape. "Go on, Howard," commanded the sergeant, getting to his feet. "I don't want to tell you again. Get over and see Doc. That's an order."

Cross struggled to his feet. "Which way?" he asked, relieved to be doing something, anything to try and figure out what had happened to him.

The sergeant pointed to his left. "Third dugout down." He shoved his hands deep in his pockets and sighed looking up into the grey sky. "Ah, shit, c'mon. I'll walk you down there. You might be in worse shape then I thought." Shaking his head, he reached down, picked up his rifle, and started slogging through the ankle deep mud towards the doctor's dug out. "C'mon, Howard," he announced over his shoulder. "I got things to do. Move your ass."

Twenty yards further down the muddy trench, the sergeant stopped and pointed to a large dugout door that was flush with the high sidewall of the trench. Sandbags at least four feet above and around the entrance gave the hole a fortress feel. A small paper red cross had been tacked to the beam above a filthy blanket that served as a door.

"Hey Doc, you in there? I have someone who needs to see ya," announced the sergeant, pulling back the blanket.

"Are there wounded?" questioned a voice inside. Cross had heard that voice before. The accent was clearly French. It was the voice from his dreams, his nightmares.

As the rain began to fall with a renewed intensity, a short bespeckled officer with a pencil thin moustache and an impossibly clean uniform stepped out from behind the blanket. He gave the sergeant a quick glance and then focused his attention on Cross.

"Doc, I need for you to take a look at Private Howard," announced the sergeant.

As the officer stepped up close, Cross could smell whisky on his breath." Are you injured, Private?"

Cross didn't know how to answer the officer with the piercing blue eyes. "I, ah, I..."

"Doc, he hasn't been right in the head since the patrol this morning," replied the Sergeant. "He isn't acting right."

The officer straightened his uniform jacket and gave the sergeant a firm stare. "And what exactly is 'acting right', as you say, supposed to look like in all this madness?"

The sergeant leaned in close to the officer, rain dripping off his nose. "Look, Doc, I didn't come here to pick a fight, okay? One of my Marines acts kind of foggy. I bring him here for you to look at. I try to watch out for my boys."

The officer held the big Marine's stare for a moment as he seemed to accept the explanation. He looked up into the rain, the droplets beading on his glasses. "I detest this war," he announced curtly to the sky. "Insanity," he turned and pulled back the blanket. "After you, Private. Watch your step."

Cross stepped into the darkness of the cave, surprised at how large the entryway was. Several candles dug into the dirt bathed the dark earthen walls in a comforting orange glow. Three steps into the entry, the passageway took a sharp left and then descended down four wide steps.

More candles helped to illuminate a large room that had a wooden floor and ceiling buttressed by a solid eight-inch beam in each corner.

There were several pieces of furniture, including a desk, a large glass-door enclosed medical instrument cabinet, benches made out of ammunition crates, and a small examining table in the room. A lantern suspended on a wire from the ceiling gave the room a strange, almost overly-bright cast.

To Cross, the room smelled like any other doctor's office he had visited. Antiseptic alcohol and the odor of wet bandages hung heavy in the air. After his eyes adjusted to the odd light, he could see large dark stains on the floor. Dried, sad islands of blood had stained the wood black, a stark and sobering testament to the carnage that was taking place above. Men had died in this room, probably many.

"Remove your tunic and have a seat on the table, Private," announced the officer, taking off his uniform jacket and rolling up his shirtsleeves. Above, a deep thudding rumble of thunder rolled overhead, announcing another miserable rainstorm. "How long have you been in France?" questioned the doctor, washing his hands in a small basin.

"I, ah, I'm not really sure, Doc."

He walked up, standing close to Cross and shined a small flashlight into his eyes. "It is not a difficult question, Private. Is it that you do not remember?"

"Doctor, I really don't know how to answer your question. I'm having trouble with this entire reality."

The Doctor stepped back giving him a curious look through the bottom of his glasses. "And what 'reality' do you think you belong in, Private?"

Cross shook his head. He could see where this was going. The officer was never going to believe him if he said anything about being someone else. "It's just I really don't think I am supposed to be here. Doctor, this is going to sound strange, but I think my name is Jim, Jim Cross and ..." His voice trailed off as he started to feel his memory fade. "I, I'm having trouble remembering a different life, I, ah."

"That's okay, Private. This war, this reality has done terrible things to men's minds. You are not the first to suffer like this."

"Cross, Jim Cross" he whispered out loud. The name seemed strange now, the memory of who and what he was beginning to fade.

Other memories, far more bright, were beginning to come into focus. A girl he once knew, a gathering of family, his family sitting around a large table, of having a farewell dinner the night before he shipped off to France. These were real. They had substance. He remembered hugging his mother at the train station the next day, the morning he left. Had everything been a dream, a vivid shock to the senses caused by a German artillery barrage? Could it be?

The officer walked over to the small writing desk and sat down. "You do know, Private, that a diagnosis of simple confusion without injury will not get you off the line."

Cross let the barely disguised accusation of malingering hang in the air for a moment. "What's that supposed to mean? You think I wanted to see a doctor? I'm just trying to tell you what's been going through my mind. I'm not trying to get out of anything. I'm just trying to understand." He slid off the table and picked up his uniform jacket. "I think we're done, Doctor. I'll figure this out on my own."

"My door is always open, Private," replied the doctor, pouring himself a small glass of whiskey. "Would you like to join me for a drink before you go?"

"I didn't think you were authorized to drink on duty in the army," questioned Cross, pulling on his uniform coat.

The officer poured a second small glass and then sat back in his chair with a sigh, "I am not in your Army, Private. Have a seat."

Cross thought for a moment as more thunder rolled over the roof of the cave outside. "Is that an order?"

The officer laughed softly while turning back to his drink. "I don't give orders, Private. I stopped trying to control this madness a long time ago. Do as you wish."

Cross walked over to the small table and sat down. The officer smiled and picked up his glass. "A toast to you, Private Howard."

Cross nodded and drank the shot down in one gulp, the warm whisky burning a hot, ragged path down his throat. He coughed and tried to get his breath as the officer smiled and poured himself a second drink.

"Jesus", coughed Cross, feeling the liquor hit his stomach like liquid fire, "That's really strong."

Before the officer could answer, the big platoon sergeant quickly walked into the room, his uniform soaked from the heavy downpour outside. "Hey, Doc," he announced, walking across the room. We're getting hit. Fritz is coming through the wire and we're about to get real busy. You done with Howard?"

The sudden sounds of rifle and machine gun fire outside on the wall stopped the conversation. "Let's go, Howard!" shouted the sergeant, tossing Cross his shotgun. "We need every swinging dick."

Cross followed the sergeant, slogging through the rain and ankle deep mud on the trench line, the heavy, familiar smell of gun smoke and cordite hanging heavy in the air. Stepping up the short ladder to his firing position, he automatically started shoving shells into the shotgun while trying to see through the smoke and rain that covered no man's land. Slowly a thousand dark silhouettes advanced across the shell-cratered ground a hundred yards away, their long bayonets and spiked helmets glistening from the rain. The primal screams and shouts of men killing and being killed filled the air as the machine guns on the trench line continued to zip hundreds of rounds into the assault. And still they kept coming.

Transfixed by the carnage, Cross watched as the German soldiers struggled through the mud and tangled barbed wire rows fifty yards away. Covering fire by German snipers began to come in as a Marine, manning a machine gun close by was suddenly jolted backwards from a bullet through the forehead, his lifeless form crumpling into the mud like a discarded rag doll.

A microsecond later another bullet zipped by Cross's cheek, snapping him back to the present. Shocked, he watched three Germans breach the wire twenty yards in front of him. They were closing fast, firing their weapons as they advanced. Cross jerked the shotgun to his shoulder and pulled the trigger. Raw terror ripped through his body as he realized he hadn't put a round into the chamber.

The men were now less then ten yards away as he racked in the rounds and fired all four twelve gauge buckshot shells in quick succession. Two of the Germans went down, while the third fell to his knees, holding the side of his face, blood pouring through his fingers. He quickly loaded two more shells, blasting the wounded soldier onto his back. The 12-gauge trench gun, at close range, was as effective as it was brutal.

Overhead, German airburst artillery detonated in brilliant orange-white flashes raining hot steel into the trench defenders below. Seeing Marines getting hit all around him, Cross jumped from his fighting and into water and mud just as a second series of airburst shells ripped through the overcast sky. The murderous barrage continued as he grabbed the body of the dead Marine and rolled it on top of him. He lay in the cold muddy swill as the dead Marine's blood dripped onto his face and neck. The barrage continued for several more minutes and then a sudden pervasive hush filled the air.

A slight breeze wafted down the trench line carrying the oddly sweet smell of blood and gore along with the low cries of the wounded. Cross slowly eased out from under the body and saw that the corpse had absorbed hundreds of pieces of German shrapnel. In death, the Marine had saved his life. Stunned, he now saw that of the six marines that were with him on the wall, he was the only one that was alive. The barrage had killed them where they stood, their bodies crumpled and torn in the mud.

He had no perception of time, no urgency to his actions as he stood in the trench trying to comprehend what had just happened. It was as if his mind could not absorb the event, the stimulus of the battle destroying any emotional ledge he had to stand on. As the rain began to fall, he slowly sank back down onto one of the ammo crates, feeling as if he had aged a thousand years. Moments later, Cross was surprised to see the big platoon sergeant, covered with mud, slide down beside him from the top of the berm.

"Jesus, Howard, you all right?" He asked looking around. "Hell of a fight, huh?"

Cross picked up his shotgun and dumped water out of the barrel, trying to think of something to say. He looked over at the Sergeant and was about to speak just as the bone-chilling scream of "Gas" echoed throughout the trench line. This was far from over.

Chapter Six

It had been four days since the stroke, four days since she had found him close to death, lying in their living room. All the medical interventions currently on the market had been used in his treatment, and he had stabilized. Now it was just a waiting game.

She had gotten to the hospital early that morning, hoping against hope, that she would see some signs of recovery, some glimmer of light in her darkness of fear and indecision.

"Good morning, Danielle." The doctor, along with a nurse pushing a cart stepped into the room. "How are you today?"

"Fine, still hopeful that he's going to come out of this."

The doctor leaned over the bed adjusting the breathing tube. "Well, he's stable. Now we just have to wait and see how he reacts to the medications."

Danielle watched the nurse draw several blood samples and adjust the oxygen flow. She moved with an air of sureness and precision that announced many years of experience. The doctor handed her the clipboard and then stroked the bottom of Jim's foot with his pen, looking for a reflex. "I'm getting some response," he said stroking the other foot. "That's a good sign."

"Have you noticed his eyes?" questioned Danielle, getting out of her chair and standing beside the bed.

"What about them?"

"They are moving a lot under his eye lids, you know, like he is dreaming, like he's in REM sleep."

The doctor leaned close to Cross's face. "Yes, I see what you mean. I'm not sure it means anything, most likely an involuntary response. Interesting though. "

As a nurse, she had seen hundreds of stroke and brain injury patients, but in all that time, she had never seen this kind of rapid and sustained eye movement. "So you're saying this is not unusual, Doctor?"

"Danielle, I am trying very hard to keep your expectations at a reasonable level. Jim has suffered massive damage from this stroke. In fact, I am stunned that he has survived this long."

Danielle thought for a moment. "I think something else is going on here."

"And what do you think is going on, Danielle? People who have had this kind of stroke very rarely, if ever, get up and have a normal life. It just does not happen."

The doctor motioned to the nurse that he was leaving. He reached over and touched her hand. She immediately withdrew. "Faith is a good thing, but we also have to look at reality. I'll check on him later this afternoon."

She brushed back a tear. "I'll tell you what, Doctor. I will take faith over this kind of reality anytime. I can't put my finger on it, but something else is going on with Jim. If he is trying to get back here, I'm going to do everything in my power to see he gets the chance. I would like a second opinion on his condition."

The doctor nodded, putting his pen back into his pocket, "That's fine. I can give you a list of some other fine neurologists. I'll leave a printout with the night nurse."

As the early evening began to settle over the city, she continued to sit by his bedside and watch the silent storm that seemed to rage just behind his closed eyelids. She worked to suppress the guilt she felt for the indifference that had grown within her towards her husband, how she had minimized his efforts to find his way. The drift between them had started small but then morphed into this expansive emotional gap, a gap that had left them both miserable.

It had taken years for her to become distant and withdrawn and only a microsecond to realize how much she really loved him. Watching the street lights come on in the hospital parking lot, she vowed that she would do everything in her power to not let him slip away. They had come too far together, been through too much, for it to end this way. "No," she told herself, 'The doctor was wrong on this one. He has to be."

***

The mortar rounds, full of deadly cargo, arched gracefully high overhead from the German lines. Up through the overcast sky, over the broken muddy field far below, and then in descent, they exploded twenty feet off the ground. To the survivors, the hushed thud of detonation did not bring panic but only annoyed observance of something that had been going on for months. Exploding shells were common on the trench line, but these shells were different, much different. They contained mustard gas, that gauzy white haze of blinding, blistering smoke, with the odd odor of onions and strong vinegar, a scent as beguiling as it was deadly. They were capable of inflicting ghastly injuries that would not heal and were terrifyingly indiscriminate.

When inhaled, the vapor immediately caused pus-filled blisters to form and bubble in the mouth, the throat and the lungs, causing the victims to suffocate in their own body fluids. The lucky ones only lost their eyesight when the gas attacked and destroyed the moist surfaces of the eyes, leaving them with a hacking cough and total blindness for the rest of their lives.

Cross was fortunate. The sergeant had been right beside him when the gas attack started. If he had spent precious seconds fumbling around with the mask, it all might have ended right there. But with the big Marine's help, he was able to get his mask on and secured just as the first wispy cloud of deadly gas quietly descended over the trench line.

The cries and curses of the Marines had filled the air as the men scrambled to get under cover and as far away from the floating scourge as possible. The soldiers' armpits, groins, necks, and any other part of the body with moisture left exposed began to blister and burn as if they had caught fire.

Cross tumbled after the sergeant, into one of the dugouts, scrambling on his hands and knees to the deepest part of the hole. There, under the suffocating mask and in nearly total darkness, Cross felt as if he had been buried alive. He fought the rising panic with the inability to draw a full breath through the crude respirator. After several interminable minutes, just as he was about to tear the mask from his face, he heard the "all-clear" shouts from further down the trench.

Fighting for control, he rolled out of the dug out, pulled the mask from his face, and breathed fresh air in great gulps. "Jesus" he gasped trying to collect himself.

The big sergeant walked up, stuffing his mask back into the canvas carrier he wore around his neck. "Takes a bit of getting used to. Stay out of the low places. Goddamned gas settles in the bottom. You get in it and stir it up, it'll burn three colors of shit out of ya, got that?"

Cross nodded, still rattled from the attack, "Yeah, yeah, I got it."

The sergeant studied him for a moment. "I need you to buck up, Howard. You ain't played out yet." With a wink and a sad smile, he wearily picked up his rifle and started walking down the trench line, to check on the rest of the Marines in the platoon.

Cross watched him slowly disappear in the fading light, humbled by the Marine's calm resolve. If there was ever a place, a tangible, solid piece of geography that one could label as hell, this was it. Sudden death floated inches above the ground, barely covering the wide-eyed, open-mouthed corpses that had settled in the mud of the trench and on the no-man's land above. The idea that he could actually die here still did not seem possible in his mind. He considered himself an unwilling observer to this hellish condition, fully expecting some unseen force to lift him up and out of this place, this time. If he was truly supposed to be here, why did he still remember a different reality, a different name?

He wiped the mud off the barrel of his shotgun as several more Marines sloshed by on their way to dinner mess. The men walking by kept their heads down, barely acknowledging his presence. The cold, the mud, and the rain had beaten them down past the point of physical fatigue. They all now seemed beyond caring for physical comfort or emotional validation of what they were doing or why. Cross had dreamed, or if he was being truthful with himself, had fantasized about doing this very thing – of being locked in a desperate battle in hellish conditions with men of equal strength and mental fortitude, of living for an undecided outcome, an outcome that would be totally dependent on a combination of herculean effort and blind luck.

He checked the chamber of the twelve gauge and fell in behind a second group of Marines that were headed to mess. As he slogged through the mud, his thoughts flew to a young redheaded woman sitting in a sunlit field of purple flowers. Ginny, her name was Ginny, and he had loved her, adored her the moment they met that warm night at the Grange dance. He had spotted her from across the room, and by the time he had worked up the courage to ask her to dance, the song the band had been playing was almost over. He remembered how she smiled in amusement when the song had ended, leaving him standing there holding her at a distance, his face red, sweat rolling down his back.

"You look like you need to sit down," she had announced, smiling.

He had nodded sheepishly and motioned towards the door. "Would you like to get some air? It's hot in here."

She had met his gaze, her green eyes bright with an inward joy. "Sure, but I can't stay out long. My father will start looking for me." She had quickly turned, leaving the intoxicating scent of Lifebuoy soap and delicate perfume in the air between them.

The memory of that wonderful night faded as quickly as it had come as he walked up to the end of the chow line. The heavy smell of bacon fat and lard filled the trench as the men opened their metal mess kits and moved down the line. The cooks quickly slapped heavy ladles full of mush into the tins, not wanting to stay on the line any longer than they had to. People got killed up here and nobody wanted to die in the mud.

As the last bit of muted sunlight faded into darkness, the flares from both sides of the line popped high above, illuminating the broken landscape in an odd golden light, a light that hid the horrors of war in dancing black shadows. Cross found a dry ledge of dirt and began to eat his food, suddenly realizing how really hungry he was. The warm, tasteless mash went down easy, giving him renewed energy with each mouthful. He quickly sopped up the rest of the gravy in the tin with the stale chunk of pumpernickel bread, wiping the plate dry.

The Marine Sergeant walked up beside him and sat down. "Goddamn, son, looks like your appetite is back. Here, I picked up some of that nasty Kraut cheese and hard tack from one of their kits. Once you get past the smell, it's pretty good."

Without a word, Cross took the food. The sergeant was right; the cheese smelled like dirty feet. "Jesus," he mumbled, sniffing the chunk.

The sergeant laughed as he lit a hand-rolled cigarette, throwing the lit match into the mud. "Now you see why them poor bastards fight so hard? They have to eat that horse shit everyday."

Cross took a big bite of the cheese, chuckling at the disgusting taste. Overhead, another flare popped into life, its golden light turning the sergeant's laughing face into a ghoulish mask. Cross forced down mouthful after mouthful of the foul tasting cheese and snort-laughed his way past the tears. He now knew that people in hell could eat and laugh while the dead and dying lay within arms reach. Now – he was truly here. He had crossed the threshold.

Chapter Seven

The Carson brothers never saw it coming that night, never even suspected that the eight o'clock domino game would lead to death by nine. They were at the top of the neighborhood food-chain, young toughs who laughed loud, talked loud, and ran heavy action against anyone that they saw as a threat. They both had graduated from petty thief status and were now fairly big-time gang-bangers in their circle of dope-slingers and protection racket thugs.

They were into their game at the back of the club as usual surrounded by sycophants and gangster wannabees, the gutless low-lifes with nowhere else to go. None of them had paid any attention to the old man as he had entered the bar. He was invisible to the crowd, written off as just some old loser with enough aluminum can cash to buy himself a beer. But as the music thumped away, the old man had slowly pulled a thirty-eight from his pocket and cocked the hammer. The Carson brothers sat slamming dominos on the table amongst a crowd of other players just thirty feet way as he drained the last bit of beer from the bottle, took a deep breath, and turned to his prey.

As Willie J stepped closer, the room suddenly seemed smaller, hotter. Sweat dripping off his nose, he moved across the crowded room, gripping the gun at his side. A second later, he stood at arm's length behind the older of the Carson brothers, the one who had tormented him the most, the one who had kicked over his cart more times than he could remember. Sitting to his right was the younger brother, the one who had raped that little Miller girl last summer but had walked because everyone refused to testify. To him, he was a worthless punk with mean eyes and a big mouth who always had something smart to say.

With a steady hand, Willie J raised the pistol and shot the older Carson in the back of the head at nearly point blank range. Instantly, the lifeless body slammed onto the table, the thirty-eight-caliber bullet blasting out just below the left eye.

The younger Carson attempted to draw the Glock 19 from his waistband in stunned surprise but took a slug through the mouth, knocking him backwards and out of his chair. Dazed and grunting in pain, he struggled to get to his feet as the old man calmly walked over and shot him three more times in the back.

The panicked crowd cleared the room in seconds, leaving a flurry of flying chairs, bar stools, and the old man standing over the dead and dying bodies of the notorious Carson brothers.

In a final bit of revenge, Willie J shoved the body of the older Carson from his chair. The corpse flopped onto its back, both eyes staring wide in sudden death. He slowly leaned over the body, pressing the thirty-eight into the man's chest. "BAM" The muffled shot made the body jump, bringing a smile to the old man's face.

"Take that one with you to hell, mother fucker," he mumbled, tossing the pistol across the room.

On his way out the door, he picked up one last cold beer from the open cooler behind the now deserted bar.

Once outside he saw people still running from the bar and getting into cars. Surprised by the panic he had created, he found his heavily stacked shopping cart and slowly started pushing his treasures home. Several police cars with lights and sirens blaring flew by as he continued to move down the tree-lined sidewalk.

The streetlights were just beginning to come on as he reached his house. More tired than he had been in years, he eased himself down slowly onto the stoop and watched as several more Detroit police units and an ambulance flashed by. Sadie Delmar, his neighbor of over twenty years, opened her screen door and stepped out onto her porch just as an unmarked car flew by. "God, Lord, looks like another killin!" she announced easing her three hundred pound bulk into one of the large metal lawn chairs.

Willie J smiled, leaning back on the step, "Yep, looks like it. Nice evening though. How are you, Miss Delmar?"

"I'm fine, Willie Jay. I got some rice on the stove if you want some."

Willie thought for a moment. "Thank you, Sadie, but I'm okay. I think I'll just sit here a bit."

Looking down the now-crowded street, he could see that one of the marked units along with an unmarked car had turned around in the middle of the block and was coming in his direction. Willie recognized Detective Kitchens as he stepped out of his car and began to move up the sidewalk. He couldn't think of a better person to surrender to. "Willie J!" shouted Kitchen, walking with his gun drawn. "You keep your hands in sight." Willie raised his hands, smiling. "You got me, Detective. No trouble here."

"Stand up, Willie. You're under arrest." The old man slowly pushed himself to his feet, feeling a strange heaviness in the chest, a fullness he had never felt before as Kitchen moved closer and snapped on the cuffs. Several uniformed officers had now arrived. "Willie, I need to read you your rights. I'm arresting you for the murder of the Carson brothers," he announced, walking him back to his car. "You have the right to remain silent. You have the right to an attorney. If you cannot afford one, an attorney will be appointed to you by the court. Do you understand what I just said, Willie?"

"Yes, Sir, but I don't need any lawyer. I shot those two because they needed to be shot."

Kitchen helped one of the uniformed officers ease Willie into the back seat of the marked unit. He leaned into the car. "So you're telling me you shot those boys?"

Willie adjusted the cuffs behind. "You're goddamned right I shot em," he announced angrily. "You want me to write it down for you or what?"

More sad than satisfied, Kitchen closed the car door. "There will be time for that later, Willie J, plenty of time." As he walked over to his car, he scanned the faces of the kids sitting on bikes, the people standing on the sidewalk and wondered how many more would have their lives ended like the Carson brothers, for that matter, like Willie J. These were his people, and as politically incorrect as it sounded, there was no white man standing in the street with a gun. Black people were killing other blacks.

Sliding behind the wheel of his car, he stared through the windshield while a light summer sprinkle began to fall. The rain did little to settle the near jubilant crowd. They laughed and screeched and hand dapped as if the arrest of Willie J and the shooting behind it were cause for some kind of macabre celebration.

Even though Willie J had been a member of the community for the last thirty years, he meant nothing to these people. He had observed this type of reaction over the years and recognized it as a product of sustained hardship and loss. The braggadocio and loudness seemed to be a way of masking the shared grief and sorrow, a collective desperation to make sense of the senseless. But the more they laughed and shouted, the more sad and hopeless things seemed to become.

A uniformed officer tapped on his window, pulling him from his thoughts. "Hey, Sarge, you want him booked down at Central District?"

Kitchen nodded, rolling his window down further. "Yes, go ahead. I'll meet you there. Book him under 750.316 - times two - for now. I'm going to have to get an official statement from him after that."

The officer looked at him curiously. "Sarge, you okay?"

Kitchen smiled. "Yeah, I'm fine. Been a long day. Going to be a long night, I'm afraid."

"Ah, do you know the suspect, Sarge?"

Kitchen nodded as the rain began to fall more heavily. "I'll meet you downtown, Officer. Better get out of the rain." He rolled up his window as the officer walked away, already feeling that persistent knot of tension in the back of his neck. Again, tonight, he would be officiating over the dismal future of another person's life from his neighborhood, a task he had now grown to hate, like serving as pallbearer at a child's funeral - necessary but terrible.

Prosecuted, bagged, or buried, they were all just numbers now. He slowly drove away from the area, not even bothering to wave back at the people on the sidewalk - kids and people he knew. He wanted nothing more to do with the living dead.

***

Cross sat cold and shivering in his damp clothes as the first rays of muted sunshine crested the eastern horizon. The Germans had pounded them throughout the night with incessant artillery, a clear indication of another pending assault. He looked down at his filthy hands and noticed that the skin on his fingers was shriveled as if he had immersed them in water, not surprising considering his current location where everything was wet, damp, or caked in mud. Even when the sun did come out, it didn't provide warmth, only a clearer view of the horror all around him.

The German dead lay in twisted, bloated heaps just in front of the endless rolls of barbwire. The rotting smell of decay drifted on the wind, making it impossible to eat or even breathe around the growing stench.

The sergeant crawled up beside him near the top of the trench, cradling his rifle. "This is a good way to get shot in the head. A sniper can get you this high on the berm. You need to get back."

Cross smiled wearily, looking at the big man. "Why do you care about me so much?"

"What?"

"I said why do you care about me so much, Sarge?"

The sergeant pulled a pair of binoculars up to his eyes and began to scan the distant German line. "I care about all the shitheads in my platoon, Private, even you."

Cross thought for a moment. "You think they will attack today?"

The sergeant stuffed the binoculars back in his bag. "Pretty much guarantee it. You're going to get another front row seat to the human condition."

Jolted by the statement, Cross stared at the big Marine. "What did you just say?"

The sergeant met his stare. "What?"

"You said I would have a front row seat to the human condition?"

"So?"

Cross leaned close, the smell of the man's cigarette-laden breath and body sweat filling the space between them. "Who the hell are you? Are you the Messenger, some kind of angel? I've heard those exact words before."

The sergeant smiled. "Listen, dumb ass, you get off the top of this trench before you get shot. Go clean your weapon and get ready to do your duty. You got that?" Cross held the sergeant's gaze. "I'm not telling you again, Private, you best get moving."

Cross slowly backed down off the bank. "I know who you are," he announced pointing at the Marine.

The sergeant smiled. "Do what you're told, Private. You'll stay alive longer."

Cross slid the rest of the way down the embankment, staring at the sergeant. "I know who you are; I'm not crazy. This is not my life, and you know it!" he shouted.

The sergeant slid down the bank and grabbed him by the front of his coat. "Listen, peckerwood, I don't know what kind of game you're playing, but it's not going to work with me. Get your head in the war, or you will not make it out of here."

Cross couldn't hold back the tears as he struggled against the sergeant's grip. "Just tell me why I'm here for God's sake," he cried. "Why this? Why now?"

The anger in the sergeant's face softened, yet his iron grip stayed firm. Cross felt his feet slowly being lifted out of the mud as the sergeant pulled him close. "You're here to be a witness," he whispered, his eyes growing dark. "Do we understand each other?"

Cross nodded, suddenly realizing that he was looking into the face of certain death. The blackness in the sergeant's eyes was terrifying. "I understand. Ah, I understand."

The sergeant eased his grip, letting him sink back down, up to his ankles in the mud. As if remembering something he had forgotten, he let go of Cross's coat and walked away without saying another word.

For Cross that was just fine. Shaken, he stood in the mud for a good five minutes, trying to get his head around what he had just seen and heard. He would do as he was told. He would do anything, even face Germans by the thousands if he didn't have to look into those eyes again.

He had no idea why he was in this new reality, no clue to his part aside from basic survival. He now had the body of a fit twenty-five-year-old Marine and if God or fate or any other ethereal force wanted him to kill Germans in 1918, then that's the way this thing would play out. He would keep his mouth shut and see what happened. Trying to analyze the surreal mechanics that had brought him here now seemed to be a waste of time.

As he slogged through the mud on his way to morning mess, the little bit of sunshine that had broken through at dawn had faded, replaced by the now familiar cold grayness. By the time he reached the end of the chow line, it had started to rain, a fitting start to another day in hell.

Chapter Eight

By the morning of the fourth day, Danielle had started to fall into a routine as it pertained to her visits to Jim's area of the ward. He had been transferred to ICU, her floor, making it convenient for her to keep tabs on his progress or lack thereof. At first the hospital administration had voiced concern about Jim receiving treatment on Danielle's unit, but after consideration of her stellar record as an ICU nurse, they had given their approval.

As part of her rounds, she monitored all of the machinery now keeping Jim alive. The ICP, a sensor attached to the skull, measured pressure within the brain. The EKG sensors monitored the heart rhythm and strength. The PEG tube provided for feeding directly into the stomach. Add the arterial line, the IVs, the catheter, and the oxygen, and Jim became lost, buried under a mass of tubing, wires, and complex equipment.

"How is his body doing?"

Startled by the voice, Danielle turned to see a large, darkly bearded man now standing on the opposite side of Jim's bed. It was if had just materialized out of thin air.

"Ah, can I help you? No one is allowed in ICU except family." She quickly looked around the ward. "Sir, how did you get in here?"

The man bent down and gently touched Jim's forehead. Alarmed, Danielle stepped forward. "Sir, don't' touch the patient," she announced firmly, trying to hide the rising fear. "Sir, I need you to leave. Please do not touch the patient."

The Messenger smiled, giving her a curious look. "I am always amazed at how protective you are of one another. I assure you that I did not come here to do any harm."

Danielle had had enough. "Orderly!" she shouted, "I need some help over here."

The Messenger smiled sadly as if reliving a melancholy memory. "I only came to tell you, Danielle, not to give up on Jim. He is on a great and difficult journey and needs you now more than ever."

"How do you know my name? How do you know Jim's name? Who are you anyway? Orderly!" she shouted again.

The Messenger stepped close. She froze where she stood. "Danielle, listen to me. The love you have for this man is transcendent. It can travel. He will feel it. It will give him strength. It will give him hope. Please remember that."

As she looked into the eyes of the big man, a large tear began to make its way down her cheek. "I, I, Why are you telling me this? Please tell me who you are?"

The Messenger gently wiped the tear away. "I am a friend, Danielle. Have faith."

Before she could speak, she suddenly felt light-headed and then could no longer stand. She slumped down, sliding down beside the bed to her knees.

"Danielle, Danielle!" Aware that someone was calling her name, she tried focus on the sound that seemed so far away, almost like an echo.

"Danielle, wake up, sweetie. Are you okay?"

She focused her eyes on the lead- nurse who was now kneeling down beside her. "Wh, what happened? What's going on?"

The nurse slowly helped her to stand. "Looks like you passed out. Did you hit your head? Are you hurt?"

"I, ah, no, I'm fine. Where did that man go?"

"What man is that?"

Danielle looked around the room, still not sure what had just happened. "He was a big man, dark beard, wearing a dark suit. You didn't see him? He was just here."

The older floor nurse gently touched her on the arm, "Danielle, why don't you go home. Get some rest. I don't think you've had a decent night sleep in days.

The nurse was right; she hadn't slept more then a few hours in days. But the fear of possibly not being by Jim's bedside if he woke up was too terrible to think about.

"Go on home, Danielle. I will call you if there is any change in Jim's condition."

"But I really need to…"

"I'm not asking, Danielle," interrupted the nurse. "I don't think you need to be on the floor treating patients in your exhausted condition."

"So, you're questioning my ability as a nurse?"

The head nurse leaned close. "Go home, sweetie. That's an order."

***

On the evening of the fifth day, Cross, along with a hundred and sixteen other Marines stood silently in the rain-soaked trench line, waiting for the artillery barrage to start before they advanced over the top. Their mission was to make it to the thick woods on the Germans' left flank, clear the dense underbrush of machine gun nests, set up a new line of defense, and then wait for French reinforcements and resupply.

The somber briefing given by the French officer had been grim with the prediction of unit success. It would be a daring move. Yet, casualty rates were expected to be high, giving every man in the assault group a sobering expectation of imminent death.

The gun, the harbinger of death that brought the most fear, was the German Maxim Gun or G80, a belt-fed, water-cooled, 135-pound man-killer with an effective range of three thousand meters, and Cross had already estimated that the German lines were no more than three hundred and fifty meters away.

The German tactic had been to place the guns slightly forward of the trench line, giving the crew a full field of fire on attacking advancing soldiers. The heavy rounds and fast cyclic rate of fire would be responsible for the deaths of thousands of French and American troops. Going over the top with Maxim guns on the other side was by definition "suicide".

According to the plan the French barrage of shot and smoke would begin at nine PM sharp, hopefully masking the Marines' unexpected flanking movement. Once the firing started it would be a mad dash through ankle deep mud and tanglefoot barbed wire for a good two hundred yards, a hellish run by anyone's definition.

"All right, listen up!" shouted the sergeant walking down the trench. "Only carry water, ammunition, and your gas mask. Drop your Haversack. We will need to move fast. I need every swinging dick in the wood-line alive. Is that clear? Once we clear the field, squad leaders, get your people together. Find out who is still with us and who isn't. Captain Travois will be conducting the regroup and assault once we hit the woods." The sergeant patted several Marines on their shoulders as he passed down the ranks. "All right, fix bayonets!" he shouted stepping up next to Cross. "Charge all weapons."

A loud "Hooah" shout went up from the ranks as the Marines fixed bayonets. Just as quickly a pervasive hush suddenly settled over the trench line as a light rain began to fall. The only sound was the tink... tink.. sound of raindrops hitting the men's steel helmets.

Soaked to the skin, shivering from adrenaline as much as he was from the cold, Cross could hear someone vomiting somewhere further down the ranks. Amber, yellowish flares tore ragged paths up into the night sky. Cross looked to his left and then right at the young men standing silently beside him and was struck by their steely resolve and dark-eyed intensity. The average age of the Marines in the trench was twenty-five, but in the intermittent light of the flares, they looked like men in their sixties. Cross felt the dread, the strange excited sickness in the gut that rolled across the ranks, drying the mouth and weakening the knees.

Quiet prayers were being whispered, sins were being confessed from the soon-to-be-dead and wounded. Cross looked over at the sergeant who was calmly lighting another of his hand-rolled cigarettes. He caught his stare and smiled. "Run fast, Marine. You can do it," he announced winking.

Before Cross could answer, the heavy thud of artillery thundered from deep behind the French lines a mile away. Immediately the high velocity shells screamed by overhead, exploding just in front and behind the German lines. "Get ready, boys!" shouted the sergeant, pulling the rifle off his shoulder. "We go on the smoke."

***

Normally Kitchen enjoyed the interview process. The routine of getting his coffee and his notepad full of case information together gave him a sense of calm, a sense of stability, just before the interview, a process that would be anything but calm and stable. Homicide investigating usually turned out to be an odd sort of catharsis for both the suspect and investigator.

There was a method in the interrogation dance. By design, the room itself was purposely small, almost intimate, giving the suspect the feeling of confinement. There were no pictures on the wall, nothing to distract attention or divert conversation. The room, kept uncomfortably cold, kept the suspect out of a normal comfort zone. The lighting, kept bright, stark, almost clinical, sent the subliminal message that nothing could be hidden. In the interview, the event would be described based on what the investigator already knew. If lucky, he would learn what he didn't know from the suspect.

Kitchen walked into the interrogation room, making sure he made eye contact with Willie J who sat handcuffed to a large steel ring that was anchored to the wall next to the table. "Those cuff's too tight?"

Willie J gently tugged against the ring. "No, Sir, need to keep a dangerous man like me in close control," he replied smiling.

Kitchen set his files on the desk and pulled out his chair. "You seem to be in a pretty good mood, Willie J, considering the trouble you're in."

The old man smiled, leaning back in his chair. "I ain't in no trouble here, Mister Kitchen. My troubles are in a bag, probably downstairs in this very building. My troubles are dead."

Kitchen shook his head. "Jesus, Willie J, you just shot two people in cold blood. Don't you know what that means?"

Willie J thought for a moment. "Mister Kitchen, I know exactly what it means. First, it means I'll never have to deal with those two sorry sons-of-bitches again. They made my life hell for years, always pushing on me, knocking over my cart, taking my cans."

"Yeah, but, Willie, you killed them for that?"

The old man leveled a hard steady gaze. "Let me tell you something, Mister Kitchen, you are gonna get old some day. And I pray you never have to live off what you find in the street. I pray you don't get pushed around because you're too old to fight back. I pray you never feel that helpless. You trying to get around to why I shot those two? Well, you live in my clothes for awhile, and you wouldn't even have to ask the question."

Kitchen sat back in his chair with a sigh, "All right, Willie J, you have anything else you want to tell me? Anything else that could help you?"

"I got nothing else to say, Detective. I did what I needed to do. Now I'm tired and I want to go lay down. Take me to a cell. I'm ready."

"So this is it, Willie J? This is how you want your statement to read?"

"Don't care how it reads, Detective. I did the world a favor by shooting them two, and you know it."

"What I know, Willie J, is that you're going to be charged with two counts of first degree murder and that ain't nothin to be happy about."

Willie J smiled. "Well, you ain't sitting on my side of the table, are you, Detective? Might see things different if you were.... One last thing before I stop talking... I'm gonna give you a Christmas present."

"A Christmas present?"

"That's right. I saw the car and the guy who shot Kojack and that other asshole, Moss."

Kitchen looked up from his notes. "How do you know that?"

"I was digging out the dumpster behind Corlito's liquor store that morning. Saw the car plain as day."

Kitchen leaned close in his chair. "Tell me what you know, Willie J. No bullshit now."

Willie shook his head. "No, sir, no bullshit. The car had the plate that said RN4EVR. Blue car. White man driving."

"How you remember that?"

"Don't know. Just something that stuck with me. Besides, ain't that many white boys riding around the neighborhood that time of the morning."

Kitchen wrote down the information. "Willie J, you're sure that's the plate number?"

Willie nodded, "Sure as I'm sitting here. Now, I'm done talking."

Kitchen closed his notebook, feeling as if he had aged twenty years. "All right, Willie J, it's been a long night. Let's go find you a bed. We'll talk again tomorrow."

Twenty minutes later he had the printout of the plate information lying on his desk. The car was registered to a James and Danielle Cross of Detroit. Neither had any warrants or arrest records. They appeared to be a normal middle-class couple. At any rate, he would find out what was going on in the morning. Right now, he needed something stiff to drink and a hot shower.

The duty officer transported Willie J to central booking without making any further statements, his defiance and resolute pride about the murders strongly intact. In Kitchen's mind, nothing else really needed to be said.

It had been a very long night, maybe the old man had it right all along - do what you have to do and to hell with the consequences. He was right on one thing for sure - until you walk a mile in another man's shoes, you don't know what you would do. "No more judgment tonight," he thought, walking out of the office and heading down stairs. He would leave that bit of cold introspection and power to the system he served.

The heavy grinding wheels of justice would turn, and Willie J would be just another black man fed into the machine. Regardless of the circumstances, his life was over, just as sure as the Carson brothers downstairs in the dark, laying ice-cold and naked in stainless steel drip-pans. Justice served? Maybe. Probably the only kind Willie J would get from the State of Michigan.

Chapter Nine

The first heavy thud of incoming artillery sounded in the distance at eleven o'clock sharp. The freight-train-sounding rush of 200-pound shells screamed over seconds later, blasting the German lines with brilliant orange and red explosions, the concussions shaking the earth and every solider to the core within 500 meters.

The shells were now falling in a steady, terrifying pattern. Suddenly, above the thunderous cacophony of sound, a faint, shrill whistle could be heard in the trench line.

"Move! Move! Move!" shouted the sergeant, climbing the short ladder leaning against the trench wall. In one large movement, the Marines surged forward, scrambling up the side, disappearing over the top of the trench.

On a dead run, Cross jumped the first knee-high strand of barbed wire and tumbled down into a large muddy crater as more covering-fire thundered in from above. For a brief second of panic he thought he was alone as he scrambled up the far side of the muddy hole before spotting at least fifty other Marines around him, running and jumping, their faces, illuminated by the ghastly orange flashes of exploding shell - locked and frozen in fearful resolve.

Cresting the rim of the crater, Cross saw the sergeant twenty yards ahead, his wide silhouette unmistakable in the flashing light. Now a good seventy-yards into no man's land, they ran forward. With thirty more yards to go before they were to turn left and run parallel to the German lines and hopefully into the relative safety of the wood line, the German trench-line opened up with sporadic machine gun fire, the heavy caliber rounds hissing and snapping by the Marines as they continued to run through the gauntlet of mud, barbed wire and shell craters. As he ran, stumbled and then ran again, Cross saw several Marines cut down, their bodies flying apart from the heavy German fire. Cross jumped the last row of barbed wire and followed several Marines now sprinting towards the wood line. A bullet zipped by his face, close enough for him to feel the heat of its flight and he jumped into a large shell hole at the edge of the woods, amazed that he was still alive. Without breaking stride, he ran up the far side and disappeared into the darkness. To his relief, he could hear Marines crashing and cursing their way through the heavy underbrush close by. He had made it.

The woods themselves had been heavily bombarded by artillery, leaving the ground covered with broken treetops and limbs. Impossible to move as a team over the tangled mass in the dark, each man stumbled through the brush, trying to hold on to weapons and gear, knowing full well that at any minute the well hidden and dug-in German machine gun nests would fully open up. The French reconnaissance reports told them that nests were positioned along the German flank to provide them with intersecting fields of fire for mutual support. As Cross slowly pushed his way through the rain soaked underbrush he could almost feel the German gunners watching his every move.

Finding a small open space of ground, he knelt down and tried to catch his breath as two more Marines moved quietly in beside him. All around, the sounds of men moving with their weapons through the tangled woods could be heard. It was a nightmare scenario; visibility was zero and the brush chocked ground made it impossible to move quietly. Everything pointed to a pending slaughter, and every Marine moving through the dark knew it.

Cross fingered the shotgun's safety, just to be sure it was ready. Suddenly, to his right he heard the bone chilling sound of a German machine gun open up with a long burst. They had found their enemy.

Cross dropped to his belly as a fusillade of German rounds snapped by, a foot over his head. He crawled several feet forward, giving him a chance to see the orange muzzle flashes from the German guns. The erratic and changing report of the weapon made him realize that the Germans were firing at sounds and not clear targets. His eyes adjusted to the dark and he could see the gun crew, a good forty yards away. He discovered several other Marines beside and behind him as they crept closer. The German fire became more frantic with long sustained bursts, shooting in all directions, as if the crew sensed the approaching assault but were blind to its direction. Now within thirty yards of the gun crew and closing, Cross began to raise his shotgun when a second German gun opened up, nearly on top of them. They had literally crawled within ten feet of a second position.

As the rounds zipped by less then a foot overhead, Cross quickly pulled one of the two grenades from his belt, jerked the pin, and tossed it as far as he could in the direction of the crew. Several seconds later the heavy KRUMPH sound echoed through the trees as the grenade detonated.

But the detonation did little to stop the now steady German machine gun fire and, to his horror, he heard a third gun open up. The Marines had crawled into a German shooting gallery.

German bullets began chewing up the wet ground close to Cross's position, throwing large divots into the air. An orange flare burst overhead and to his horror, Cross could suddenly see the true depth of the German defenses. In the brief sputtering light, he counted six machine gun nests within less than a hundred yards. He could see the dull glint of German helmets in the dying light, slick from the rain.

There was nothing he could do, nothing that would save his life if the men now hunched over their guns a hundred meters away decided to take it. At that moment he felt an over-powering sense of exhilarating freedom. His life and all the seconds, minutes and hours that made up his existence had dropped him on the doorstep of eternity - were it could soon be over.

Whatever action he took within the next ten seconds or the next ten minutes would have little to no bearing on his survival. It was a feeling that seemed to sweep through the heart and mind of every Marine who lay in the mud as the last bit of orange flare light sputtered and then disappeared back into darkness. Without any external command the Marines suddenly jumped to their feet and ran with weapons blazing straight into the guns.

Cross rolled to his feet and in three strides was at a full out sprint, a primal scream clearing his throat as he ran faster then he had ever run before. White-hot tracer rounds from the German guns zipped and snapped by his face and head and still he charged.

He moved as if he could see the rounds coming, ducking and dodging the bullets going by. In a flurry of action, now twenty feet away from the first position, he fired his pump shotgun, sending a spray of buckshot into the kneeling crew. The men spun away from the hits in agony as he closed the last several yards. Jumping into the pit, he pulled the forty-five from his belt holster, and in quick succession shot all three Germans in the head. Killing the men felt as natural as if he were stepping on an insect or taking a drink of cool water.

Stunned that he was still alive and almost giddy with emotional abandon, he quickly reloaded the M2 and swung the weapon to his left, putting a full burst into the unsuspecting German crew fifty yards away. Several more flares ripped into the night sky revealing a pitched, close-quarter battle taking place on the muddy ground below.

The Marines were now at nearly pointblank range of the German nests, well within the reach of a bayonet. The mud covered combatants slashed, shot and cut into one another with unbridled rage.

Cross ran towards the next gun emplacement, the sounds and screams of men fighting and dying in the dark filling the air all around him. As he stumbled through the underbrush, a dark shape off to his right suddenly seemed to materialize out of the ground and slammed into his legs with a driving tackle.

As he punched, kicked and struggled to get to his feet, Cross dropped his shotgun. Panicked at not having a weapon in his hand, he was able to draw his pistol just as the German found his rifle and fired. Like being punched or struck in the chest with a very heavy bag of sand, the blow lifted Cross off his feet and dropped him with a groan ten feet away.

He was instantly more tired, strangely sleepy, than he had ever been before as he struggled to sit up. In a confused state, he was half aware of a German solider standing over him. A second later he disappeared in an explosion of blinding white light.

***

"Mister Cross? Open your eyes. Jim, can you hear me? Squeeze my finger if you can hear me. C'mon, Jim, wake up." Cross could hear the voice. It sounded far away like someone talking at the far end of a concrete tunnel. He could breathe but felt as if he were chocking. He attempted to speak, trying to push through the fog.

"Easy, Jim, you have a breathing tube in your throat. Relax, now," announced the voice. "Squeeze my finger if you understand."

His vision began to clear a bit and he could make out the face of a stranger leaning close. He could smell the coffee on the man's breath.

"Jim, my name is Doctor Gains. Squeeze my finger once for yes and twice for no. Do you understand me?"

Cross tried to swallow but his throat had never felt so dry. He weakly squeezed the doctor's finger. The room began to grow brighter.

"Very good, Jim. Try and keep your eyes open. Are you in pain?"

Cross squeezed twice. His eyes began to focus on a woman standing beside the bed to his left and suddenly a pang of recognition struck his heart when she leaned close.

"Jim, it's me, Danielle. Can you hear me?" He squeezed her finger once, still trying to figure out who she was.

"Jim, do you know where you are?"

He squeezed her finger twice.

"You're in the hospital. You have been asleep for a few days now."

His vision finally cleared, yet he still had no idea who the woman was. Her voice was familiar but her face was that of a stranger.

"Jim, we need to keep the breathing tube in for just a bit longer," announced the doctor. "We have to be sure you can breathe on your own."

Cross nodded weakly, trying to make sense of what was going on. The change in the reality from where he had been to the present was overwhelming. He closed his eyes, trying to understand. Just as he was about to drift off to sleep, a heavy jolt to the chest jarred him fully awake and he suddenly found himself sitting up, the sounds of battle thundering around him.

"Goddamn, Marine," shouted the sergeant, sliding to the ground beside him. "Took one right in the chest. You were lucky; the buckle on your gas mask bag saved your life." He pulled Cross to his feet. "C'mon Killer. The Krauts are falling back; we've got to get to the rally point."

Dazed and totally confused, he picked up his shotgun and stumbled slowly through the dark after the big sergeant, as they made their way through the heavy underbrush and broken tree limbs. Overhead, flares were going off as a light rain began to fall. Below, the air hung heavy with the smell of blood, gun smoke, and cordite. He was back.

Chapter Ten

It was early in the evening when Danielle got home from the hospital, heartbroken that Jim had slipped back into a coma. It had been crushing to see the terrified, confused look on his face when he had awakened for that short time. The doctor had calmly explained to her that this kind of set-back was common with those having a deep brain injury. He had reinforced his surprise that Jim was doing as well as he was.

It had been cold comfort as she had looked into the eyes of the man she had fallen in love with and married a lifetime of memories ago. She had been haunted by the cold emptiness of the eyes, much like the gaze of a doll, as they followed her movements. The Jim she knew had not come back. The body had awakened, but she sensed that the soul was absent.

She poured a second glass of wine and tried to think of what she should do next. She was exhausted and really needed sleep but knew if she didn't shower and wash her hair now, she would just have to do it in the morning. Funny, how the little easy things in her life had become real chores since Jim's stroke. Eating, showering, and washing clothes were endeavors of annoyance now, things that took time away from his bedside. She needed to be near him, afraid that if he woke up and she was not there, that he would suffer more emotional and physical damage.

As she undressed and turned on the shower, she recognized that what she was really feeling was guilt - guilt for emotionally and physically shutting down months before the stroke. They had drifted apart and had been living separate lives under the same roof, talking without any depth about anything other than how miserable they had become. Even that repeated conversation consistently ended with door slamming, prolonged silence, and a fog of tolerated indifference that grew thicker by the day.

After showering, she slumped onto the couch with her third glass of wine, intent on letting the alcohol work its magic. Even if it was only for a brief moment, she just wanted to forget the life-changing awfulness of the stroke, to numb herself for a short time in an effort not to think about tomorrow and the overwhelming challenges that would surely come. With a practiced professional coolness, the doctor had told her that Jim's care would be long term. There would be rest homes, tube-feeding, encompassing all the drama of caring for an infant without the reward of growth and maturity.

In her mind she was constantly comparing the images of Jim as a healthy, robust, seemingly invincible man, to the tube-fed, silent wreck of a person he had become. The transformation had been stunning.

She downed the last bit of port and cursed the fleeting thought of Jim being better off dead. She wasn't a praying person, never felt the need to earnestly ask a higher power for help, yet tonight, alone in her living room, she felt the need to reach out. "Please, God, help him. Bring him back," she whispered. "I love him." She quickly brushed away a tear as the wine and fatigue of the day began to hammer away. Within minutes, she was asleep.

The Messenger stood within arm's reach, quietly watching her breathe. He had overheard her prayer. Desperation, fear, and an inability to see the larger plan always drove them to their knees. He was amazed that at these times, they still reached out to the unknown, to things far bigger than themselves. He knelt down close, watching her nostrils slightly flare as she slept. "If they only knew the truth," he thought, turning away, "they would be amazed."

***

It was nothing more than a wild guess that made Kitchen pick the Henry Ford Medical Center in the heart of downtown as the first place to start looking for the registered owner of the Blue Chevy with the license plate RN4EVR. He had run the plate and the vehicle came back registered to a woman by the name of Danielle Cross. There had been no physical address listed, only a Post Office box. But on a hunch, he had guessed she was working at one of the eight major hospitals in Detroit as opposed to a private clinic somewhere else in the city.

Even though he currently had several other open homicide investigations on his desk, every one of them important and demanding his attention, this one, this double murder carried out with measurable precision had peaked his interest. The idea that an unknown white male had been coming down into the bad part of town and had smoked two of the neighborhood's heavy players was something way outside the lines.

He pulled into the visitor's section of the parking lot as a light rain began to fall. He quickly downed three more antacids. The heartburn was really kicking his ass today. He had awakened with an odd toothache this morning, chalking it up to the loose filling he had been sucking on for days.

As he walked through the brightly lit hospital lobby, he had the strangest sensation that he was being watched, even followed. It seemed as if there were shapes and shadows that were moving parallel to his path, just on the edge of his peripheral vision.

He walked up to the main nurse's station, trying to shake the growing unease. He hated hospitals. The sounds, the smells, and the hushed, subdued manner everyone seemed to live under announced that bad things were happening here - final things, hard choices, and permanent goodbyes. The hospitals all looked the same and, for him, they all carried the same level of clinical dread. He had watched his older brother die from cancer in a hospital. It had been a slow agonizing death that killed him in small increments over the course of a year. Chemo, radiation, experimental drugs, all did little to nothing to stop the assault. The two hundred and thirty pound man who had been a running back for two years at the University of Tennessee, had wasted away to a ninety-five-pound wraith of his former self, buried in a junior sized coffin.

Even four years after his brother's death, Kitchen had to suppress the urge to vomit whenever he smelled children's bubble gum because it carried the same odor as the disinfectant used in the cancer ward. To Kitchen, it would forever be the smell of pending death.

"Excuse, ah, I'm detective Kitchen, and I was checking to see if a Danielle Cross works here?"

The young nurse sitting behind the counter with the nametag that read "Penny" hung up the phone. A quick cloud of fear crossed her face. "Annie? Danielle Cross? Yes, she works here. Everybody calls her Annie. Is there some kind of trouble?"

Kitchen put his badge back in his coat pocket. "No, I just need to get some information. Is she around?"

The nurse thought for a moment. "No, she doesn't come on til four this afternoon. She works in ICU."

Kitchen took out his handkerchief and dabbed his brow. "Is it hot in here or is it just me?" He was feeling worse by the minute.

The nurse slid a small piece of paper across the counter. "This is her cell number. I'm sure she has it on. Detective, are you okay?"

"Yes, I'm fine. Just have a headache. Thank you for the number. I'll give her a call."

As he left the nursing station, the pain in his jaw began to radiate down his left arm making his fingers tingle. As he walked, the length of the hall seeming longer than before, a rivulet of sweat ran down his back. "Just a few more steps," he thought, "and then I'll be out in the fresh air. Just a few more steps."

The volunteers who manned the hospital's information desk later told the police officers that the detective had walked to the automatic doors and stood there for a moment before dropping to the ground without saying a word.

Being just yards away from the ER, two physicians had been at his side in moments. Within the span of sixteen minutes he had died twice only to be brought back by the defibrillator. In a short time, he had been rushed into the OR where a triple bypass procedure saved his life. In the time frame of six hours, his life had changed forever.

Surrounded by an array of sophisticated heart monitoring equipment and other machinery now keeping him alive, Kitchen slowly opened his eyes, trying to fight off the crushing fatigue and sleepiness. He didn't recognize the large bearded white man that was now leaning close.

"How are you feeling, Detective?" he asked smiling. "Probably not too well I suspect."

Unable to speak Kitchen nodded weakly. Within the next breath, he was asleep.

The Messenger gently patted him on the hand and then looked over at Cross, resting, almost invisible in the middle of his own array of life support machinery less than twenty feet away.

A nurse walked into the ward and stopped, startled to see the man standing by the detective's bed. "Sir, you're not supposed to be in here," she announced as she approached him.

The Messenger smiled. "I'm just leaving."

Sensing something oddly foreboding about the man, the nurse kept her distance as he walked past her and stepped into the hallway. Feeling as if she should say something or alert someone else, she pushed her way through the double doors and was surprised to find the hallway empty. The man had vanished. Confused, she stopped at the nurse's station. "Did you see the bearded guy walk by here?"

The nurse looked up from her paperwork. "What guy?"

"He was huge, well over six feet, black suit, black shirt and tie, dark beard. You had to have seen him?"

"No one has come by here, Stacy. Didn't see a soul."

Outside, the rain had picked up, the temperature dropped twenty degrees, - odd for this time of year. To the Messenger, the weather meant little. It was never a factor as it related to the tasks he had to do.

He enjoyed walking among them and was careful with his manner, including his speech and the way he dressed. "They would be terrified if they saw him as he really was." It had been mandated at the beginning that the two worlds should only meet in death. Even then, great care had to be used.

The emotional displacement in death was the most powerful thing "they" would ever go through. If the process was not conducted with the mandated attention and care, the individual might never recover; the emotional balance could be destroyed. Because they had no real sense of "forever", a measure of time very familiar to the Messenger, nothing could be left to chance.

As he walked through the rain, he was struck by how peaceful the city had become. As a rule "they" didn't like the rain, ran from it, protecting themselves with umbrellas, newspapers, just about anything that would shield them. To the Messenger, rain meant renewal, a chance to wipe the slate clean, to make things right. He took comfort in the fact that some of them saw rain for what it really was, a gift, a possession of the divine - truly an enlightened point of view.

If anyone on Kessler Avenue had been paying attention to the big man in the dark suit walking in the rain, they might have noticed that despite the heavy downpour, the man's clothes stayed dry. It was unusual to say the least. But then again, a lot of unusual things happened in Detroit.

Downtown at night, the vibe ran the gamut from ignorant bliss to full-blown car-jack panic when a wrong turn was made. Being careless in the city after dark was just asking for it. To the Messenger, Detroit was his kind of human city - hard on the senses, interesting to observe.

The Messenger drew an odd sort of comfort knowing he wasn't the only one of his kind in town. The Shades were everywhere. He could smell them. He knew they followed at a distance, waiting, watching for an opportunity - a moment of weakness. In that moment, with every bit of their rage and strength, they would try to destroy him. Before vanishing into the night air, he stopped and listened to the footsteps coming close, movement only he could hear.

"Hashuka, Sidqa, Wayli," he shouted to the thick shadow. The ancient Aramaic warning stopped the Shade ten feet away. The shadow shimmered and then condensed into the definable figure of a short, neatly dressed man. The Messenger had not seen this one before. To the casual observer, he appeared to be a man in his late fifties having a thin build. Wire-rimmed glasses gave him the look of a banker.

The Shade stood motionless, staring intently, his face totally void of any emotion. "I don't know you," he announced in perfect Aramaic.

The Messenger stepped closer, his form growing to his full height. "If you wish to be ended, I will accommodate you."

The Shade smiled without humor. "We shall see, Dumaya. We shall see." Without another word, he vanished.

"Strange that the Shade had called him by his title," he thought walking away. In all his conflicts - warfare with the beings, his name had never been announced. Something was very different about this Hashuka, something very different indeed.

Chapter Eleven

It had been two days since Cross's unit assaulted the German machinegun emplacements on the far left flank of their position. The operation was a stunning success, but the cost had been horrendous. Of the two hundred and sixteen Marines that went over the top that fateful night, eighty-seven had been killed, sixty-two wounded. Less than fifty men survived unscathed yet would now carry the indelible memories of murderous, point blank combat in the mud and rain.

During the fighting, Cross had lost his trench gun. He now sat on an empty ammo-crate, half asleep just after sunrise, cradling a German Mauser rifle.

"You keeping that as a souvenir?" question the sergeant wearily lighting one of his hand-rolled cigarettes.

He, along with half a squad of mud-spattered, bone-tired Marines, had just finished the first hot breakfast they had had in days and were now sitting near the mess bunker trying to catch some rare morning sun.

"I lost my shotgun. Picked this up this morning."

The sergeant motioned for him to hand it over. Cross wearily tossed the rifle. The sergeant checked the bolt, working the action several times. "Not bad. Think you can hit anything with it?" he asked tossing the weapon back.

Cross was in no mood for casual banter. His chest was extremely sore, making it hard to draw a full breath and the pounding headache and crushing fatigue only made him want to sleep. He slowly got to his feet, feeling the worn out back and leg muscles throb from the effort. "I'll be in my hole, I have to sleep. Wake me up when we start killing people."

Without waiting for permission or even a reply, he slogged off in the direction of his dugout. He could give a red piss what the sergeant said; he was too exhausted to do anything other than find a relatively dry patch of ground and collapse. For the rest of the morning and well into the afternoon, it seemed that both sides were so grateful for the blue sky and sunshine that neither fired a shot. It was as if all the collective rage of war had temporarily been expended the night before. The dead had been removed, the wounded treated and evacuated, leaving the exhausted soldiers from both sides quietly pondering their fates.

Cross had stumbled into his dugout that morning and slept six hours without moving. He woke to the smells and sounds of the mess crew ladling out the nightly stew of boiled potatoes and bacon fat.

Painfully, he got to his knees and then slowly stood up, his body aching as if he had been in some kind of high-speed vehicle crash. "Jesus," he whispered, stepping out into the trench to follow several Marines on their way to chow.

"Ain't no Jesus here," mumbled one of the Marines walking by. Cross fell in behind the men, grateful that it was still quiet and that it wasn't raining.

As he walked through the ankle deep mud, a flash of memory almost made him stop in midstride. It was a soft, peaceful image of two large German Shepherd dogs running across a neatly trimmed lawn on a bright sunny day. Why would the memory of dogs give him a faint yet perceptible pain just above his heart? He stopped and looked up into the leaden-grey sky realizing that they were his dogs. The memory was part of another life, another event in the mind of a man with a different name. He trudged up to the end of the chow line, lost in a blur of disjointed fragments of images of people and places.

"Glad you're back with us, Marine." Cross turned to the voice behind him. "Lucky the rats didn't chew your lips off - being asleep that long," announced the sergeant, blowing a lung full of hand-rolled cigarette smoke in the air.

"How is it that you're never very far away from me?" questioned Cross, locking his gaze on the man. He needed answers and was now in no mood to have his questions brushed aside. "I mean, seriously, what am I doing here?"

The sergeant smiled. "You're starting to scare me again there, Private. Thought you would feel better after your beauty sleep."

"Listen, Sergeant, I can feel how cold and wet my feet are. I can feel how wet and heavy this wool coat is, and I can feel the grit between my teeth from the mud I am standing in. But you and I both know that I am not supposed to be here and that I am someone other than the person named on my ID card. So let's just cut the bullshit. You seem to be a major part of this thing that's happening to me and I need to know why."

The sergeant nodded, indicating that the chow line was moving. "You think I have all the answers?"

Cross took several steps forward before answering. "I know you have all the answers, Sergeant. I don't think anything happens here without you controlling it somehow.

The big man laughed. "So I am God now? Boy, there's a promotion a fella could get behind! Is that what you're getting to?"

"That's exactly what I'm saying," snapped Cross, angrily facing the sergeant. "Why don't you cut the crap and tell me who or what you really are?"

The sergeant leaned close, his nose, now inches away. "What I am, Private, is someone who is really hungry, and if you don't move, I'm gonna knock your dick in the dirt."

Cross stepped back and quickly pulled the forty-five from his holster. "You do what you have to do you son-of-a-bitch," he replied, racking the slide. "My name is Jim Cross, and I am a sixty-year-old man living in the year 2014. Now, I'll bet if I shoot you in the goddamned forehead, I might just get back to where I am supposed to be. What do you think?" He raised the weapon, thumbing back the hammer. "Let's find out."

In the microsecond of time between the decision of blowing the big sergeant's brains out and the time it took to squeeze the trigger, a thunderous explosion roared up from the ground, thirty yards from where they stood. The incredible over-pressure of the detonation blew everyone within a hundred meters in every direction off their feet. The blast had lifted both Cross and the sergeant out of the deep trench, dropping them ten yards into no-man's land.

As the smoke cleared, Cross slowly got to his knees, trying to catch his breath and clear the muted ringing in his ears. The sergeant lay motionless, face down in the mud, several feet away. Still not realizing the gravity of their situation, Cross stumbled over to the Marine.

He grabbed the man's shoulder. "Get up, Asshole!" he shouted, rolling the sergeant onto his back. "We have unfinished....." he fell back on the ground, stunned by what he saw, unable to speak. From the chest up, the sergeant's face, neck, and most of his head had been blasted away, leaving a pulpy pink mass of shredded flesh and brain matter in the mud. What was left was unidentifiable as a human being.

Rifle and machinegun fire suddenly erupted all around him snapping him out of his shock. He frantically crab-walked backward through the mud and wire, trying to get to cover. Strong hands jerked him back into the trench seconds later just as a bullet grazed his chin. He was safe. Trying to make sense of what had happened, he picked up his rifle from the mud and slogged his way back up to the side of the trench where remnants of his platoon were now firing at a steady rate.

"What happened?" he shouted to the Marine, frantically loading the big Browning machine gun.

"Kruats dug a goddamned tunnel under us. Blew up half the company!" shouted the Marine, slamming down the feed tray.

Cross looked to his left at the huge crater that was once part of the fortified trench they had been living in for the last three months. The hole was still smoking. Severed arms, legs, and twisted piles of gore lay scattered in the mud, a jarring testament to the severity of the blast.

"Here they come!" shouted one of the men. Cross looked toward the German lines and was stunned to see at least a thousand troops streaming across no-man's land. This was an assault in broad daylight and, by the look of it, they intended to overrun the Marines' position. He knew instantly that there was no way the line would hold. The German assault was just too large.

***

"Am I dying?"

"Yes."

"Will this hurt?"

"No, your pain is over, Son. I am here to help you through."

Kitchen knew at that moment that he would be all right. The voice from the light was familiar, a voice of calm assuredness giving him the strength to let go. He could hear the sound of wind blowing softly, like it would through a screen door on a warm summer day. It was the sound of his youth.

He was aware of the sequence of events that had brought him to this point. The nagging sickness hours before the heart attack, the disjointed, visual fragments of hurried medical staff working to save his life. And now this, the time of his death had arrived. In the soft hazy light he could see but not discern a form, a shape.

"I thought I was getting better," he whispered, already knowing the reply.

"You were getting worse. The damage was too great. Are you ready? There is nothing to fear."

Kitchen slowly reached out to the shape and, to his surprise, his long-dead father stepped out of the haze and gently took his hand. "My son," he whispered.

Kitchen let the tears fall. "I've missed you so much, Pop."

"I know, Son," replied the man, gently patting his shoulder. "I have been with you all along. We are all so proud of the man you were. You've done very well with the time you had."

Kitchen could feel the coolness of the glass floor on his bare feet while the pleasant warmth of a gentle breeze seemed to come from every direction at once. The pain in his chest was gone and his senses never more alive. "I'm ready, Pop."

The older man smiled. "Okay, Son, let's go home."

The floor nurse heard the heart monitor alarm go off and was at his bedside in less than a minute. The doctor had been making his morning rounds and was in the hall when he heard the alarm. Even as he orchestrated the final dance of crash cart, adrenalin push, and all the rest of the actions that bring an arrested patient back from the abyss, he knew in his heart that this one was gone.

After ten minutes of frantic effort from the entire crash team, the doctor stepped back from the bed, shaking his head. "I'm gonna call it," he announced, checking the digital clock above the bed. "Nine seventeen. Joan, will you log the time, please?"

The nurse noted the time on the chart and began turning off the monitors. "I really thought he was getting better," she said, turning off the large overhead examination light. The doctor leaned over the body with a small penlight, checking the pupils one last time.

The Messenger stood at the back of the room watching the nurses and doctor perform the ritual of the dead. They spoke in muted tones, their movements deliberate but almost as if they were unsure of what to do next. There was awkwardness in their manner in death, directly opposite to how they reacted to the injured living.

The Messenger was always intrigued by how the witnesses acted when confronted by this final truth. They avoided looking at the body, quickly covering the face with a sheet. After death, the process of removal was swift. Orderlies were called, logs were closed and the room was cleaned - all with machine-like precision. The quicker the reminder of their own mortalities was removed the better.

"This one had been easy," thought the Messenger, leaving as quietly as he had come. He had been able to shield the transition of the Detective from the Shade, knowing full well that many battles still lay ahead.

The death of Detective Kitchen barely made the paper –a picture of a young graduate from the Police Academy in his graduation uniform sent to the paper by the last remaining family member, his younger brother. The smiling young man at the beginning of his career was in stark contrast to the beaten down sixty-year-old man he had become.

His fellow officers at the station had hosted the wake, toasted his passing with sad good-byes and heart-felt stories of their time with the man. He would be missed. But if the lines of communication were suddenly opened between the living and the dead and Kitchen were asked if he would like to return to the life he once lived, he would smile and say - "Not in a million years, my friends, not in a million years."

Chapter Twelve

The letters had stopped coming weeks ago. The building tension of not knowing was the worst of it. A telegram announcing a wounding or even, God forbid, a battlefield death would be better than having no word at all. Margaret Ginny Stiller sat on her bed on her mother's expansive porch writing her second letter of the day. She had torn up the first, embarrassed by her anger and the petulance within the prose. She was angry at his silence, angry with the war, and angry that he had so readily volunteered. She had railed that many of her friends had found and married respectable men. The fact that some were now starting families only heightened her anxiety about the future. She would be twenty-three next month and, according to her mother, would be well into the years when respectable women begin having children.

A sudden hot gust of wind carrying the smell of fresh cut alfalfa wafted across the porch. July in Ohio was always hot, the heat and humidity staying well into September. Earlier in the summer, her mother had moved all the beds onto the screened-in porch, a yearly ritual due to difficulty sleeping in an overly warm house at night.

Holding her papers tight against the breeze, she listened to the sound of her mother beating the rugs that hung on the line in the back yard, knowing that any minute she would be called to help with the endless list of household chores.

Margaret lived in the expansive house with her brother and older sister along with her mother and father, Bill Stiller, one of the town's three prominent civil attorneys. Her brother, Kyle, had taken an internship in New York that summer with one of her father's law school classmates, a prestigious opportunity.

Her older sister, Jane, worked in her father's law office as a secretary, having no real inclination for the law other than earning money for what she really wanted, which was a sailboat, an odd thing to wish for if you were a young woman in Hamilton, Ohio, in 1918. Nonetheless, Jane had fallen in love with the sea and was determined to spend a good part of her life exploring it. Even though she had never actually seen the ocean, she had read every book and newspaper article about seafaring adventures and had listened with total attention to the retired whaling captain as he lectured at her school just before her graduation. She now longed to see its expanse and would do everything in her power to save the money her father paid her, even though her mother thought her dreams of the sea were unrealistic if not down right odd.

Margaret had other plans, other desires. She had fallen in love with Bristol Howard's oldest son, Jonathon, the oldest of three brothers and had been swept off her feet the moment she had laid eyes on him at the Grange Hall Dance a year and a half ago. The Howards were farmers, making a hard scrabble living off the land with nothing to look forward to other than hard labor and short money, but Margaret and Jonathon had grown inseparable over time, taking long walks through the woods and fields, talking about anything and everything. Life together had held all the promise either could imagine, and both intuitively knew that they had found a great treasure in one another.

The summer of 1918 had been unusually hot, bringing with it a nightmarish swarm of grasshoppers that had devastated the wheat crop. Many of the small farms in and around Hamilton had gone under, leaving many families destitute. As an attorney, Bill Stiller had handled the bankruptcy of several of the local farmers, an endeavor that did not endear him to the general population. In fact, it could be said that the locals disliked him almost as much as the banks.

That dislike and tension had come to a head in late August, six months after Jonathon had shipped out for France. According to witnesses, Bill Stiller had just left his office when a drunken man approached him with an axe. The man, one of the local farmers who had lost his farm to the bank, began to accuse Stiller of working with the bank to take his land. It was an accusation that carried some weight, as Stiller had taken over the land note two weeks after the foreclosure for a small fee, legal - but opportunistic in the eyes of the towns' people.

The argument carried from the front of Stiller's law office and into the street where it took a deadly turn. Stiller had done his best to calm the man. But after dodging several swings of the axe, he pulled a small thirty-two-caliber pistol from his coat pocket and shot the man through the head. Even though the shooting was later ruled a clear-cut case of self-defense, no one in town looked at big Bill Stiller the same way after that terrible day. One of their own had been shot down by someone who already had the reputation of being "quick with the pencil", local vernacular for shady business practices. Now, the Stiller family as a whole was suffering the quiet animosity from the community, the killing having painted all of them with the same brush.

It now seemed that Margaret's world of money and family influence was falling apart, and it had been a month since any letter had arrived from France. She had written in her second letter to Jonathon of her love, about all the things she wanted to do when he got home. She had told him of the shooting and all the difficulties that had come with it. She had shared her deepest longings, and now she hadn't heard from him. She would not allow the idea to settle in her mind that he could be dead somewhere. A Just God, in all His mercy, would not allow that to happen. When he came home, they would build a life together. Nothing would get in their way. She vowed that she would marry him no matter what her mother said. No one was going to stand in the way of their plans.

***

The first wave of German troops had charged into and over the wire only to be stopped mere feet from the American trench, hundreds cut down by the three remaining Browning belt-fed machine guns. Enough suppressive fire had been put down in the middle of the American line to allow the second wave of Germans to break through. Cross and the remaining hundred and sixty battle-weary Marines suddenly found themselves in a bloody melee of close quarter combat.

Cross fired his last shot from his rifle as a German soldier twice his size slammed into him, knocking him off the top of the trench and into the mud below. He quickly rolled onto his side, pulling his pistol as the German leapt off the top of the parapet in an attempt to spear him to the ground with his bayoneted rifle. Cross shot the mud-covered German in mid-air, his body thudding lifeless onto the ground.

Getting to his feet, he emptied his pistol into three more Germans who had broken through and were now running down the middle of the trench firing their rifles. Just as he knelt and loaded another magazine into his forty-five, a hot stinging punch slammed into the back of his left shoulder, spinning him to the ground. Dazed by the bullet, he rolled onto his back and was horrified to see a German soldier less then five feet away ripping the bolt back on his rifle. Cross raised his weapon and both men fired at the same moment. The German fell back, the heavy round crashing through his face as Cross felt a deep burn zip through his right thigh just below the groin. In less than a minute he had been shot twice and now lay immobilized in the mud bleeding to death. All around him men from both sides cut, slashed and shot each other in bloody point-blank combat.

Twice, a dead man dropped onto him, pinning him deeper into the mud. In agony he desperately tried using his good arm to push off the weight of the bodies, only to be bayoneted through the cheek by a German soldier who was running by. He felt the blade skid across his teeth. He tasted the iron as it ripped his lower gum and pushed through the side of his neck. Shear adrenalin drove him to struggle to his knees and crawl to the entrance of a large dugout in the side of the trench. A crushing fatigue was growing by the second. With the last of his strength, he rolled into the darkness of the hole, letting the sounds of battle drift away in a fog of heavy unconsciousness.

***

It had now been a full three and a half weeks since Jim's stroke, and the doctors agreed he was stable enough to be moved from ICU and into a general ward. Although he was still in a deep coma, he was breathing on his own - a good sign. The Messenger had stayed close, knowing full well that the Shade was planning, watching everything. He knew they never made a move until the odds were in their favor.

For the second time, Cross felt a strange movement as though through a cloud. The voice of the Messenger was propelling him through time and space, but as suddenly as it had begun, the movement stopped. This time he didn't feel the terrifying sense of falling. Instead, there was a soft transition from dark to light as if he was waking up from a peaceful sleep. He found himself sitting under a large white marble archway, reaching hundreds of feet into the sky.

The light was clear and bright, giving every object and skin-tone an odd, nearly translucent glow. Cross could feel the coolness of the smooth stone as he sat trying to mentally absorb his surroundings. He noticed that he was wearing a dark brown uniform of sorts - devoid of stripes or ribbons but immaculately clean and perfectly tailored. Moments later a figure seemed to appear out of the glowing light, its shape and walk familiar.

"Hello, Jim," announced the figure, walking up.

He was a man, dressed in a similar uniform with short-cropped silver-grey hair. His skin was deeply tanned, giving him the appearance of robust health and strength. "How you doing, my friend?" questioned the man, extending his hand.

Cross shook hands as he stood up. "What is happening?"

The man laughed, "Well you see, Jim, that's why I'm here - to explain a few things."

"Am I dead?"

"Oh, no, Jim, far from it. You're just in transition." The man gently nudged Cross's elbow, indicating that he wanted to walk. "You see, Jim, death, as you perceive it, is a very complicated issue. It has many different facets and several different endings."

"I really don't understand any of this. If I am not dead, then where am I? This feels very real to me."

The man laughed again as they continued to walk. "Oh, this is real, Jim, probably the most real thing you will ever encounter. You see, my friend, you are in transition."

"Transition?"

"Absolutely. You see, every being, every soul has a path to follow. Some have more paths to follow than others before they become the beings they are supposed to be."

Cross stopped walking. "You're talking about reincarnation? Is that what this is?"

The man shook his head. "No, Jim, you are as you have always been. You have just been given chances in material life in order to perfect the being you are destined to be. As I said, it takes time."

"Is there a God? Are you God?"

The man stopped and smiled. "There is a God, Jim, and He is wonderful. But, no, I am not Him. I'm just a foot soldier who is here to move you on."

Cross pondered the statement before speaking. "What am I?" he asked softly.

"Ah, now we're getting somewhere, Jim. You're a soldier, always have been. You see, my friend, you are being groomed, as it were, honed and tested by trial and tribulation, pain and suffering, so you will be ready."

"Ready for what?"

The man stopped. "For the greatest gift any being can receive. There is no higher calling. You're going to be a Messenger."

Cross shook his head. "I, I don't understand. Who are you? What is your name? And why was I chosen?"

The man smiled. "You can call me Mike. And as

to the 'why' - it is not for me to know, only that it has been decided, and for the rest of your natural life, you will be preparing for that time."

Cross felt his heart skip a beat as a million questions flashed through his mind. "You're Michael! You're an angel! You're Michael - the Archangel!"

The man smiled. "Feel better now? I'm called a lot of things, Jim. Never really have gotten used to that title."

Cross didn't know where to start. "Ah, what, I mean is - where are your wings, the halo, the huge sword, all the other stuff? You know, the flowing robes and all? Isn't that how angels are supposed to dress?"

The man laughed loud and hard. After a moment he collected himself. "Ah, sorry to disappoint you, Jim, " he replied, wiping a joyful tear from his eyes. "You're talking about all the Baroque paintings and Renaissance stuff. Gosh, it's amazing how much those images stuck with the public."

"So, none of it is true? You don't have wings? There is no war against good and evil?"

The man's face seemed to cloud over with concern. "On the contrary, my friend, there is a very real struggle against good and evil, and it is deadly. It's far more complicated and dangerous than you know."

"So, why am I here? Why are you telling me this?"

"That's the exciting part, Jim. It's time for you to reflect, see where you've been, see where you're going. It's also a time for you to face a difficult truth."

They stopped walking and were now standing by a small, crystal clear stream surrounded by large smooth stones and thick green grass. To Jim it was the most beautiful spot he had ever seen.

"Have a seat, Jim." The man motioned towards a small log bench near the water. As they sat, he pointed to the stream. "Take a look, Jim. What do you see? Go ahead."

Cross leaned closer, slowly watching clear visual pictures of his life come into focus. He saw himself walking across a compound in Iraq as a security consultant years earlier. The picture faded in the stream and then a scene emerged of him riding in a truck when he worked in Africa. "What is this?" he whispered, mesmerized by the images.

The man smiled. "It's your life, Jim. It's where you have been. It's a record of what you have done. Everything is recorded."

The images then shifted to him in the trench

line in France, shooting his shotgun and running through the barbwire. "How can I be doing this during this time? I was born in the fifties? I don't understand."

The man leaned forward. "Ah, now you see - that's the tricky part. There is physical birth and a spiritual birth, two very different things, my friend. There is also physical war and spiritual war. You see, all of us have a destiny, a state of fulfillment that needs to be achieved. Look at the water. You'll see what I mean."

The images were now of him sitting in his wife's car in Detroit, suddenly engaged in the lethal gunfight with the two men that were trying to rob him.

"Not pretty is it?"

Cross felt a deep sense of remorse as he watched the bloody shooting. "Will I be punished for this?" he asked, looking at the man.

The man smiled, "Don't you think you have been?" He motioned back to the water. "What do you call that?" The images changed, showing him laying in the muddy dugout in the trench line, slowly bleeding to death. "I'd say that was a form of fairly severe punishment, wouldn't you?"

Cross sat back on the bench as the realization of what the man was telling him started to become clear. "So, you're are telling me that there are consequences for all of our actions. Is that right? Every action we take has an effect on something in the future."

The man patted him gently on the shoulder. "That's right, my friend. Everything we do in life affects something else. We can choose any direction, and there are many. But they all come with a cost and consequences. Now, you have more to see. Look in the stream. Who is that woman, and what is she to you?"

Cross watched the image of Danielle's face drift by. "That's Danielle. She's my wife. We've been married for ten years." As he watched the stream, another image came into view of a different woman. Surprised that he knew her name, he whispered, "Margaret, that's Margaret. How, I, I mean, why do I know this woman?"

She is within another path, Jim, part of your journey to the place you are supposed to be."

Cross thought for a moment. "Am I supposed to choose between these two? Is that it?"

The man stood up and walked down close to the stream. "You already have, Jim. You made it out of France. Your body didn't die in that muddy hole. Several hours after the German assault, the French counter-attacked. They found you, and you were sent back to a field hospital in Paris. You're due to be shipped home tomorrow on a hospital ship."

"What about Danielle? We are in love? Doesn't that count?"

The man looked back and smiled. "You're referring to the 'love conquers all' thing aren't you?"

"Yes, of course. That's exactly what I'm talking about. What about our relationship?"

The man walked back up and sat down. "Well, that's the tricky part about all this, my friend. As you said, there is a cost in all the decisions we make. You made a decision while you were married to Danielle, a decision that resulted in the death of two men. There is a cost for that decision, a consequence, and in your case one that is quite severe."

Cross was stunned. "So, what are you saying?"

The man stood up and extended his hand. "What I am saying, Jim, is that you survived France but you did not survive the stroke. There was also a deep emotional death in the marriage, an injury that cannot be healed. Time to go, my friend."

Cross slowly stood up. "So this is punishment for that? I lose my wife? I lose everything I worked for? Is that it? You know, I remember everything. I prayed for years to get a break. I could not find work. What about the consequences of that? Where's the justice in that?" He was now working hard to control his anger. "I'm just supposed to forget the woman I spent ten years of my life with? That's not right. It's not even remotely fair. What about all the prayers? Don't they count? I called out for help a thousand times and nothing happened. What about that?"

"Jim, listen to me," replied the man stepping up close. "You have been given a great gift. You have no choice; you have to move on. Some things are hidden. We don't know why - they just are."

"Well, that's great - pretty good loophole for not getting an answer to prayers. That only leads to the conclusion that 'the God you serve is unjust.' What happened to all the talk about mercy and forgiveness? Was all that a lie?" questioned Cross angrily. "My wife does not deserve to be hurt like this. We have a life together. We have plans. This isn't right."

"I am sorry you feel that way, Jim, but you have to know that everyone is on a path to their own destiny, even Danielle. Have you given it a thought that your death moves her to a greater awareness, a higher level that she would never have reached if you were there? She loves you,

Jim, and will always love you, but she also has a path to follow. This is happening the way it is supposed to happen. No one here is trying to hurt you. These things happen, my friend, because you made choices. It has to be this way."

The man put his arm around his shoulder. "Jim, the compassion of a Just God is to give you the ability and strength to go through the travail and all the pain. A Just God would never remove the opportunity for you to get stronger, for you to grow. Do you understand? I know this is not easy. There is a natural balance that has to be restored."

"I, I, think I do," he replied, fighting back the tears. At that moment he knew the man was right. He remembered thinking after several days had gone by after the shooting that he had gotten away with it clean, no witnesses. Well, now he knew the price he was about to pay. All actions have consequences, indeed. "Will I remember my life with her? Will I remember anything?"

The man held his gaze. "No, but you will have moments when you will sense your past. A sound, a smell, even a person's face will stir a distant memory of something that could not have happened."

Cross thought for a moment, resigned to the

fact that he would never see Danielle again. "Will she be all right?" It was more of a plea than a question.

The man smiled, his shape fading into the light "Yes, she will be fine, my friend. She will be fine."

The last thing he saw was the man reaching over and touching his forehead...and then he saw nothing at all. Little did he know that an epic battle would soon be waged on his behalf. Beings that had been alive for centuries would cease to exist. This time a great price would be paid for a decision he did not make.

Chapter Thirteen

The Messenger had been sitting in the booth for the last half hour, nursing a drink he could not taste, watching the well-dressed man at the bar laughing and talking loudly with several young women. Growing tired of the show, the Messenger snapped his fingers. The man at the bar suddenly stood up, straightened his tie, and excused himself from the female company. He picked up his drink from the bar and walked over to where the Messenger was sitting.

"I don't like being summoned," he sneered, taking a drink.

"Sit down, Deama. I'll get right to the point."

The man snorted a reply and slid into the booth on the opposite side of the table. "Make it fast, Death Dealer. I have things to do. And speak English; I'm tired of listening to Aramaic." He raised his glass as he smiled at the females at the bar.

The Messenger locked an icy stare on the Shade. "I will only warn you once. Jim Cross is moving on. He has been chosen and will not be meddled with by you or any of your minions. You're wasting your time being here. Leave this one alone."

The Shade downed the last of his drink, studying the expressionless face of the Messenger. "What makes him so special, Death Dealer? He is just another weak, highly-flawed human. You know, I am always amazed at the 'talent' your side calls up for bigger and better things. Fucking amazing."

"Don't push the issue, Deama. Do not interfere. You won't get another warning. I've only given you this one because of our past. This is going to happen."

The Shade slid out of the booth and leaned across the table, his eyes black with barely-controlled rage. "Don't ever talk to me about the past. I didn't recognize you at first, but now I do, and I owe you nothing. Threaten me again, Messenger, and I will tear you, this building, and everyone in it into tiny little pieces. I will take what I want when I choose to take it. Oh, yeah, and you tell Mike that I know about his little talk with 'our boy.' Did you really think that we were just going to let this happen? Let one more of them move into your ranks without a fight? You know exactly how this is going to end. Gonna be fun."

The room grew quiet as the few patrons still inside looked over at the two men, sensing that something was very wrong between them. The Shade adjusted his wire-rimmed glasses and then tossed his drink on the floor while motioning for the women. "C'mon ladies. Party's moving."

It was everything the Messenger could do to not leave his seat and kill the Shade as he walked away with his female companions. The hatred between the two sides was almost an entity in itself. It permeated the room like a bad smell. It was a struggle that had been waged for thousands of years through countless battles and untold slaughter. The next meeting would not be so cordial.

After several minutes, the Messenger left his seat and walked out into the early evening air just as the streetlights were coming on. He quickly fell into step with the foot-traffic passing by. Commuters were now on their way home on foot, in cars, on bicycles, all distracted by I-phones, ear buds, and all the other modern day gadgets that stole attention, making it easy to walk among them without notice. A block and a half down the street, no one saw the large bearded man in the dark suit vanish into thin air. Amazing!

***

Danielle had arrived at the hospital at eight-thirty, planning on meeting the hospice representative at ten. She had planned to go over the final plans for moving Jim to a constant-care facility closer to her home. The last several days had shown little to no improvement in Jim's condition, a heart-breaking realization for Danielle who honestly had thought he was getting better. Since he was now breathing on his own, there was no real need for him to stay on the ward and risk any complications of infections or other hospital-borne respiratory issues. As she was going over the charts from the night shift admittances, Penny, walked out of the ICU ward.

"Penny, did we have a death on the ward?" she asked, flipping through the charts.

"Oh, that's right, you haven't been here since Friday. A detective had a heart attack downstairs, but he died on Sunday. Really sad. He seemed like a nice man."

"You said he was a police officer?" questioned Danielle. "What was he doing downstairs?"

Penny sat down behind the large nurses station counter. "Didn't he call you? He was up here that day asking about you."

Feeling a sudden ball of fear roll in her stomach, Danielle sat down in the other desk chair. "Why was he asking about me? What did he want?"

"Don't know. He just asked if a Danielle Cross worked here. I gave him your number and then he left."

"Jesus, Penny, you gave him my number? Why would you do that?"

A look of confusion and surprise clouded the young nurse's face. "Danielle, he was a police officer. He was asking about you and I thought it was important. What, did I do something wrong? Are you in some kind of trouble?"

Danielle forced a smile. "No, not that I know of. So, he didn't say what he wanted to see me about?"

Penny could see that Danielle was upset about the police asking about her. "No, he just asked if you worked here and then he left. Maybe you should call the police and find out what he wanted."

Danielle thought for a moment. "Yeah, you're right. I'll call after I check on Jim."

Penny opened the desk drawer. "Wait a minute. I just remembered, I put his card in here. Yep, here it is - Detective Kitchen." She handed the card over.

Tentatively, Danielle took the card as if it were on fire. There was no way in hell she was going to call the police. Intuitively she knew it somehow involved Jim, and the last thing she needed now was more trouble. She put the card in her pocket, more determined than ever to protect Jim as much as she could. *Whatever he had done or whatever he had been involved with prior to the stroke was minor in comparison to what they had to deal with now.*

***

"Why is this happening? I can't take much more of this."

Jim, you are going through a very difficult transition but one that is glorious when completed," replied the voice from the fog. 'It starts - now."

Instantly, the light changed from a hazy warm fog to a bright clear day. He was now standing on a high bluff overlooking an expansive forest-covered valley. A cool breeze welled up from the tress below carrying the scent of pine. The clarity of the air and the brilliance of the sun were nearly overpowering. He had never seen such a magnificent landscape.

"I am interested in your opinion?" announced a voice behind him.

Cross turned and was stunned to see a large man, well over seven feet tall, clothed in what appeared to be Roman style Armor. He was carrying a large round shield of highly polished bronze and a sword in the other hand that was nearly as long as his leg. His breastplate and helmet were highly polished metal and glinted like spun gold in the bright sunlight. A long, deep-purple cape attached to the shoulders of the armor nearly touched the ground at the man's heels. It was a magnificent display.

As the man stepped closer, Cross was shocked by the man's face. "You're, you're dead. I saw you die... I saw you die in France," announced Cross, stepping back.

The armor-clad soldier laughed. "Tell me what you saw, Jim. I'm sure you have a million questions."

Cross looked into the familiar face of the sergeant. "I saw you get blown apart in the trench that day. I saw what was left of your body."

The man smiled while sliding his sword back into a metal lined sheath that hung from his belt. "What you saw was an exit, Jim. You had gone as far as you were going to go. The explosion was my way of leaving. It was for your benefit. Great care is taken in these tests and trials so that what is being presented does not overwhelm your ability to deal with the situation, whatever that may be."

For Cross, it was a jarring revelation. "What does all this mean?" he asked pointing to the valley behind him. "Why am I here? Why is this happening?"

The man held his gaze for a moment and then reached into a small leather bag attached to his belt. He pulled out what looked like a small crimson colored stone. "Take this. Swallow it. It will help you understand."

Cross took the stone, noticing that it was warm to the touch and weighed almost nothing. "What is this?"

The man smiled. "The reason we are all here," he whispered.

Cross held the stone up between his fingers, studying its brilliance through the sun. He looked at the man a second and then swallowed the stone. He was surprised that it dissolved the instant it hit his tongue. Sensing something was happening to his vision and his body in general, he looked up into the face of the man as tears began to roll down his cheeks. "It...It tastes like... like blood."

The man smiled. "Exactly," he replied, patting Cross on the shoulder.

Cross suddenly dropped to his knees, sobbing uncontrollably. Every action of deceit or selfish word he had spoken or committed during his entire life seemed to flow from his body in the tears. He saw it all in his mind as scene after agonizing scene flashed by. All the self-serving things he had done in private, all the lies he had told, all the pain he had caused others during his life pounded away, flowing out of his body as if he had been shot a thousand times. Just as he thought he couldn't stand anymore, the images of his callousness and disregard for others increased. More lies were exposed. More injuries were revealed. On it went until he lay on the ground, exhausted and spent, no longer able to shed another tear. He struggled to catch his breath as the man helped him to his feet. "Now do you understand, Jim?"

"Yes," he whispered, nodding, still trying to collect himself. Astonished, Cross discovered that he was now standing in front of hundreds if not thousands of armor-clad soldiers, dressed nearly identical to the sergeant. Thousands of breastplates, helmets and shields gleamed in the sun like jewels. "How many are they?" he asked, still trying to comprehend what he was seeing.

"Seventy times seventy times seven, a number that should be sufficient."

After composing himself, Cross stepped closer to the man. "Tell me why I am here, Sergeant. Please, no more riddles."

The Warrior nodded. "Have you ever wondered where warrior angels come from?"

"Well, I thought that when a believer dies, he joins God's army. At least that's what I heard in Sunday school."

The Warrior laughed. "I really wish it was that easy, my friend. No, Jim, soldiers such as myself and the ones you see here come from a race of men who have been chosen before they are physically born. They are groomed in life, tested and tried by hardship and war. Those are the beings that guard the gates of what you call Heaven."

"So what happens to the ones who die that aren't chosen for this task?"

The Angel smiled. "They go home, Jim. They go home."

Cross-thought for a moment. "So this is a pretty big honor, huh?"

The Angel, along with several others in the ranks, laughed. "Yes, Jim. It's a pretty big deal."

Cross looked down surprised to see that he was now wearing the same kind of breastplate and short leather tunic as the others. "I have to ask. Why aren't you using weapons from the 20th century - swords and shields? It doesn't make sense."

The Angel smiled. "Jim, what are all the 20th century weapons and armor made of?"

Cross thought for a moment. "Steel, iron, magnesium, gun powder."

"Exactly, all things made from the earth, clay and soil, the same substances you are made of, my friend. That is why they are so effective against your kind. We are spiritual beings, Jim, as you are at the moment, and only weapons forged in the spiritual realm are effective here."

Cross looked down and saw that a large, slightly curved sword now hung at his side. "Explain the gear," he asked, examining the weapon, its blade - a bluish-silver color with an edge as sharp as any razor.

"The Sword is the Truth personified, able to separate all lies. The Shield is your Faith, faith that what you are doing is right and just. The Breastplate guards the heart so it cannot be stolen or swayed. The Helmet is protection of the mind. The armor of the warrior is power."

Cross sheathed the sword. "And the stone that tasted like blood?"

The Angel paused, as a look of deep melancholy clouded his face. "Sacrifice," he whispered softly. "Sacrifice."

Chapter Fourteen

It would be the last time she would be checking on Jim in the Critical Care Ward. He would be moved to a hospice facility later that day. She had been rattled by Penny's news. The fact that police had come by to ask about her was a clear indication that Jim's stroke was only one of several problems she currently faced. She forced herself to take a deep breath and relax, not wanting to carry any negative energy into Jim's room. She would figure out how to deal with the police later.

Walking into his room, she immediately had a sense that something was not right. The atmosphere felt odd, warm, as if a great number of people had just been inside, leaving their body heat and smell behind. She opened the drapes and turned down the thermostat, trying to relieve the gloom. Walking up to the side of his bed, she was alarmed to see that his breathing was shallow and the eye movements were very active as if he were in deep REM sleep. She checked his pulse and was shocked at how weak it was. Panicked, she pushed the nurse's station "call button". Something was terribly wrong. His color had turned from pale to death-grey in minutes.

***

Cross picked up the heavy shield and helmet that lay at his feet. The Angel stepped close and fastened the chinstrap on Cross's helmet. "Are you ready for this, Jim?"

Cross nodded. "What do I do?"

The Angel pointed his sword towards the valley. "That is the Valley of Gideon. We have to cross it."

Cross turned and looked out over the expanse. Peering closer, he noticed that the breeze had stopped, but the brush and some of the small trees continued to shake from an unseen force. Something was moving in the wood line. "What's down there?" he questioned, already knowing the answer.

The Angel picked up his shield, his face locked in a cold gaze. "Your test, Jim, the hardest challenge you will ever face. Thousands have gone before you. Thousands have failed. I want you to fight the fear that you are feeling right now. As it has been written, *God has not given us the spirit of fear, but of peace and joy and a sound mind*. Hang onto those words, Jim."

Cross looked up at the Angel and then back to the woods. "You haven't told me what's down there or why I have to do this?"

The Angel kept his gaze on the valley below, his voice nearly a whisper. "Every Warrior has to prove himself worthy of his position. It has been this way since before time began. Everything you fear, everything you have run from your entire life, is down there waiting to destroy you. It has to be confronted."

Cross was stunned. "I don't understand. How do I fight things like that? And does everyone who dies get a second chance?"

"No," replied the Angel. "Only warriors in life, those who have been killed by the Shade, get a chance to take a second path. A chance is given to those whose time in life was cut short."

The Angel slowly raised his sword and the ranks of warriors standing quietly by, took two steps forward.

***

Danielle pulled back the bed sheet looking to see if the heart monitor pads attached to Jim's chest had come loose. The monitor was registering borderline fibrillation. One of the attending physicians walked in as Danielle checked Jim's pulse. "What's going on?" he asked, stepping up close to the bed.

Danielle was on the verge of tears. "I, I don't know. I just came in and found him like this. He's barely breathing, and I'm having a hard time getting his pulse."

The doctor quickly pulled a plastic oxygen mask off the tank and put it on Jim's face. "Danielle, get me a thirty-cc push of adrenalin. Also, let's get a blood gas on him." He bent close, raising Jim's eyelids while shining a small penlight. "Pupils are fixed, non-responsive," he announced, turning on the portable defibrillator.

***

"I am half your size," replied Cross, still wanting answers. "If what is down there is as big as you, I don't have a chance."

The Warrior smiled. "We are with you, my friend. We are your guardians. We will be with you every step of the way. Your job is to run like you have never run, fight like you have never fought, and when you think your strength has failed you, fight on. We will be at your side."

Accepting the response, Cross slowly pulled the sword from the sheath, surprised at how light it felt in his hand. He tightened his grip on the shield straps, pulling it close to his body. He nodded to the Angel who was now standing beside him." Okay, I'm ready. Let's go."

***

The heart monitor above the bed suddenly sounded a single consistent tone, as did several other brain wave and fluid monitors arranged around Jim's bed. In a flurry of activity, the attending nurses, the doctor and Danielle readied drugs, readjusted monitors, all following the script the dying dictated. Rubbing the lubricated paddles, the doctor announced "Clear". The dull thump sound of electricity shooting through Jim's body did nothing to the flat-line heart monitor.

***

Cross stepped off the lip of the ridge with sword and shield in hand realizing that this was the battle of his dreams and the subconscious origin of his nightmares. Looking over his shoulder, he saw rank after rank of armor-clad Warrior Angels stepping down the ridge with him. As he continued to walk, he felt the dirt and sand gather between his toes and the leather of the sandals. He noted the growing coolness of the thick, dark woods ahead. As if sensing his thoughts, the warrior walking beside him spoke in a hushed tone. "Hell can be a cold place, my friend."

***

The Doctor pressed the paddles a second time and then a third time to Jim's chest as Danielle shook with silent sobs. She watched her Jim slip away.

The eye movements stopped and the familiar yellowish -grey color of death rolled slowly down the body, from his head to his chest. The doctor checked the pupils one last time. "I'm sorry, Danielle," he said, stepping back from the bed. "He's gone."

***

Cross stopped in midstride as an odd, never-before-felt sensation suddenly coursed through his body. It was as if he had been chained to the ground by heavy shackles that had suddenly fallen off. The feeling was exhilarating, yet strangely sad at the same time. A heavy pang of loss hit his heart and then disappeared, replaced by a feeling of intense joy. He looked back at the ridge that now seemed to be miles behind him. "You've crossed the threshold, Jim," announced the Angel smiling. "You're following the path. Get ready. They are waiting."

***

Danielle didn't know what to feel as she stood beside Jim's body. Sorrow, pain, an overpowering sense of loss.... everything seemed to hit at once. They had been together for ten years, and in the span of three weeks he was gone forever. In the week prior to the stroke they seemed to have had nothing to talk about. There had been nothing even resembling a normal conversation, only arguments and slamming doors. Now, she would give everything she had just to hear his voice.

She numbly sat down beside the bed thinking about the last few days they had together... his strange story about how his pistol was destroyed and his meeting an Angel. She remembered the day of his stroke and how crazy he had been acting about his cell phone. Maybe all those irrational behaviors had been due to a physical problem in his brain.

"Danielle, I am so sorry," announced Penny walking into the room. Several other nurses walked in behind her and stood close to the bed. "Danielle, honey, we need to get you out of here so they can move Jim. Okay?" She hugged Danielle again and slowly moved her away from the bed as several other nurses moved with them. "I'm okay," she replied, dabbing her eyes. "I just can't believe he's gone. I just can't."

As the small, sad entourage slowly moved down the hall, the Messenger stood at the foot of Jim's bed studying the lifeless face. It was moments like this when he most wanted to tell the survivors that this was not the end. He wanted to reassure them that even though it seemed like an ending at the time, this was not the final good-bye. He felt their grief, their pain and their suffering and had deep compassion for their mourning. He was relieved that the Shade had not appeared at the moment of Jim's passing. He knew Jim was in Gideon's Valley and suspected the Shade would throw everything he had into the fight there.

The Messenger thought back to his time, his test in that horrendous valley. The fight for his existence had seemed to go on for days. It was a bloody, visceral experience that every potential legion member had to go through, a challenge of spirit and body above all challenges.

As he walked out of the hospital, he could sense the presence of the Shade nearby. A cold breeze had come up carrying the unmistakable stench. "I know you're here, Deama," he announced, walking down the sidewalk. "Your smell marks you." There was no reply, only the noise of the late afternoon traffic going by. The Messenger knew the Shade would strike when he felt the odds were in his favor, a predictable trait with something that was anything but predictable.

Chapter Fifteen

As Cross moved deeper into the shaded woods, a smell started to rise up from the ground, more foul than any odor he had ever encountered in his life. "What is that smell? "he whispered to the Warrior, who was walking close by.

"The blood of a million saints. The ground is soaked in it." Cross looked down at his feet and discovered that a brackish, crimson liquid was oozing between his toes. It felt as if he were walking on a thick, water-soaked carpet.

Peering through the gloom, he started to see large dark shapes moving silently through the underbrush. They were still too far away for him to see what they were, but their movement was increasing, as if they were all running to a fixed position somewhere up ahead.

He suddenly felt a strong hand on his shoulder. It was the Legion leader. "They are here. They will come from two sides," he whispered. "Steady."

A split second later a thunderous roar echoed through the treetops as the sound of a thousand beings began crashing through the underbrush. The Legion of Angels immediately formed a phalanx, shoulder-to-shoulder in front of Cross just as the howling tide of red-and-black-clad demons slammed into the Legion shields. The impact rocked the line of Warriors in a thunderclap explosion of sword wielding combat. The sound of the fight was incredible.

Cross was stunned by the ferocity and rage of the attackers. Their black armor and shields flashed and glinted in the subdued light of the forest. Both sides slashed and chopped each other to pieces as a second wave roared up on the left flank, mere yards away. Again, the Legion quickly formed an impenetrable wall of sword and shield.

"Move forward!" shouted the Angel. "Do not stop!"

Cross had never experienced such terror, such over-powering dread as he moved behind the line. All around him, armor-clad beings who existed in the darkest regions of hell and nightmares, dove, jumped, and spun into the Legion with increasing intensity and uncontrolled rage.

The Legion slowly began to push the howling, slashing hoard backward as a third wave of demons, at least a thousand strong, slammed into the rear guard. The slow-moving enclave was now surrounded.

Suddenly, several Shades slashed their way through the ranks on the right side of the phalanx. At a dead run, they hurled themselves directly at Cross. In less then a second, they slammed into his shield, taking him off his feet and into a whirling, sword-flashing melee of unbridled murder.

For a split second he looked into the cold green eyes of one of his attackers and immediately felt an icy shiver of doubt flash through his mind. *I am inadequate. I am unprepared for the challenge. I am less than nothing, and I could fail.* Just as quickly as the thought shot through his mind, it was gone. He parried a second blow and, with all his strength, swung his sword low, severing both legs of the demon in a spray of foul-smelling crimson.

Suddenly, the large Warrior Angel was at his side, smashing his sword into the attackers with lightning speed, their blood spraying across his armor. "Run!" he shouted above the melee. "Follow the ranks." Stumbling through the dead and dying, Cross fell in behind the advancing line of angels who were slowly cutting a gruesome swath of death through the trees. The sound of their swords and the crash of their shields reverberated throughout the forest like a giant killing machine with a thousand flashing blades cutting down everything in its path. Even as they were in the throes of death, the demons thrashed and swung daggers and swords toward him as he ran by, his bronze shin guards now dented and scarred by the countless sword strikes.

As he continued to swing his blade at hundreds of wounded, Cross felt his strength begin to fade causing him to fall further behind. Tripping and falling to his knees, he suddenly felt a heavy hit from the back that drove him into the mud. A searing pain of unimaginable intensity flashed through his shoulder as he fought to get to his feet. Summoning strength, he spun around and found that he was inches away from his attacker. Brilliant green eyes of unbridled hatred stared through the slits in the demon's helmet. Again, the eyes sent the message of doubt into Cross's soul. *I am unworthy of the sacrifice, a failure at everything I've tried in life and, now, in death.*

Refusing to accept the message, a primal scream came up from the depths of his being as he slammed his shield into the Shade, while swinging his sword in a wide arch, a blow that landed solidly on the side of the demon's neck, nearly severing the head from the body. Reeling from the deep dagger-wound to his shoulder, he stumbled to catch up with the ever-advancing ranks of the Legion. Blood, his blood, now ran down his arm, making the sword handle slippery in his hand.

The Legion leader was at his side as he stumbled and ran, shouting a passage of scripture that Cross had heard as a child. *Thou shall not be afraid for the terror by night, nor for the arrow that flieth in the day. Nor for the pestilence that walketh in darkness, nor the destruction that wasteth at noonday.* At the last second, Cross saw the shadow overhead and dove to his left just as a large winged-demon cleared the Legion line, landing nearly on top of him. The Beast thudded into the soft ground and with one leaping bound, crashed into him with enough force to knock the shield from his arm and the helmet from his head.

He tumbled into the underbrush, still clutching his sword, as the Shade slashed and flailed the ground all around him. Cross rolled to his feet swinging with all his might, connecting a glancing blow on the demon's shield. He staggered backwards as the Shade lunged forward, his heavy sword skipping off his breastplate. As he continued to parry and deflect the Shade's blow after powerful blow, Cross could see that the Legion was drawing further away in the drive to exterminate the demon force, a fact not lost on his immediate adversary. Unexpectedly, the Shade suddenly stopped his assault, leaving Cross breathless and confused as to why the attack was broken off.

With the sounds of battle fading, the Demon slowly stood to his full, eight-foot height. He took several steps to his left, his bright, hate-filled green eyes staring intently. "Well, Jim, look's like you're just about done. Are you ready to die?"

Cross was stunned and sickened. The voice coming from the Shade was that of his father. The demon continued to circle as Cross tried to deal with a new wave of heart-splitting emotions. His father had died years ago from a sudden and totally unexpected heart attack, an event that had shaken everyone who had known him to the core. He had no history of heart disease or any other major health condition for that matter. One minute he was fixing his lawn mower in the garage on a bright, early July morning. The next moment he was dead on the floor.

"You're not real!" shouted Cross fighting back the tears. "You're not here."

The Beast laughed a bone-chilling hack. "Oh, I'm real all right, you sniveling piece of shit. Don't you recognize your old man?"

Cross swung his sword at the head of the Shade and missed as the demon ducked and then countered with a jump-kick to the chest, slamming him to the ground. "C'mon, boy. You can do better than that," laughed the Shade continuing to circle his prey. "You were always a disappointment to your worthless mother and me. I should have drowned you when you were five. Would have done the world a favor."

Hearing the taunts and insults in his father's voice cut Cross deeper than any sword or dagger. The emotional pain was incredible. "No!" he screamed, lunging at the Shade. "You're not real!" The demon sidestepped the attack while delivering a sharp, vicious blow to the side of his head. The Shade then grabbed the back of Cross's armor and ripped it from his body, throwing him to the ground. "C'mon, tough guy, show your old man what a real bad ass you are!" he shouted. "You're not hurt, are you, boy?"

Fighting to stay conscious, Cross crawled on his hands and knees through the blood-soaked mud, fully-expecting a sword blade through the back of the neck at any moment.

Exhausted, he rolled onto his back in time to see the Shade quickly approaching, his sword held high with both hands, ready to strike. Suddenly, out of the corner of his eye, he saw a blinding, thunder-clap-flash of light strike the Shade with such force as to cut him in half. The top portion of the body simply disappeared in a red mist, leaving the legs standing, and then falling over in midstride.

Bleeding and battered, Cross forced himself to his knees, trying to comprehend what had just happened. All around him were the sounds of hurried movement and the deep rushing roar of a strong wind. Struggling to stand, he let the fear go, surrendered to whatever power had appeared and resigned himself to the fate that had arrived in the whirlwind. As the wind died down, a sudden hush permeated the air as if the molecules in the atmosphere that carried sound had evaporated. A second later, he heard the sound of something flying through the sky at great speed.

He looked up just as a large winged-man literally dropped out of the sky with a heavy thud, landing a short distance away. The man was dressed in a darker than coal-black breastplate and shield while holding a large, semi-curved sword of near translucent silver and a Spartan-like helmet of black onyx with long black, silver-tipped sharply-pointed horns.

Cross guessed his height to be well over seven feet as the Being turned and walked in his direction. Expansive black wings suddenly folded up behind the man and then disappeared all together. The Being exuded an air of total awareness and lethal power, a physical personification of war and nightmarish dread. Cross could not control his trembling as the imposing warrior took several steps in his direction. Shaking, he held up his broken sword, preparing for the final, brief fight that would end it all. There was no way he could defeat the massive creature that now stood silently before him. It was over. All the struggle, all the pain, had come down to this last emotionally crushing moment.

"C'mon, finish it!" he shouted, stepping forward. The Warrior kept his silence. "C'mon!" screamed Cross. "Fight, finish this! I'm ready."

With stunned surprise, Cross watched as the being suddenly dropped his shield and slowly removed his helmet. "So my friend, you want to fight me?" questioned the Angel, smiling. It was Michael. With over-whelming relief, Cross dropped his broken sword in the mud and sank to his knees. From the combination of crushing fatigue and blood loss, he could no longer stand.

The Arc Angel stepped up placing his hand on Cross's bowed head. "You test is over, Jim. You have fought well and have found great favor."

Cross looked up into the face of the Warrior, wiping the blood and sweat from his eyes. "What do I do now?" he whispered.

The Arc Angel smiled. "You rest, Jim, at least for a season."

Cross slowly pulled himself to his feet, with the help of angels. "And then what?" he asked. High overhead, in the fading light of sunset, Cross could now see hundreds, maybe thousands, of winged warriors circling, watching, and guarding.

Michael laughed. "And then, you come home, Jim. You come home. You have earned your place in our ranks." With his vision starting to dim, Cross looked over his shoulder and noticed that much of the Legion that had walked with him into the valley had reformed the ranks and were now silently watching him. The fighting was over. The Shade had left the fight. He looked back at the Warrior with tears in his eyes. "Will I remember this? Any of it?" he asked, already knowing the answer.

The Arc Angel shook his head. "No, but you will sense that something wonderful, something extraordinary has happened to you. You will live the rest of your days knowing that there is a force for mercy and love far greater than anything in the world."

"When does it start?" whispered Cross, falling into the soft, heavy folds of unconsciousness. A strong, yet reassuring voice lifted him through the fog. He recognized it as a voice that gave him great comfort. "It starts now, my son. It starts now."

Chapter Sixteen

The Messenger sat on the ledge of the building watching the movement of the city far below. It was one of his favorite spots, a place of solitude and peace in a city where peace and emotional solitude were at a premium. He was now a witness to the human feeding-frenzy currently taking place in Detroit, something that had been going on for years. It was both interesting and incredibly sad at the same time - watching the slow but steady decline of the city's soul. As he watched the late afternoon rain-clouds slowly drift in over the city, he was heartened by the news that one of his charges had crossed the valley, had survived the ordeal, and had now secured a spot among the ranks of the Legion.

"Sounds like your boy made it."

The Messenger turned to the voice and discovered the Shade standing a short distance away. "I got a chance to catch the tail-end of things. It looked like Mike saved the day for your guy."

The Messenger, wary of the Shade's appearance, stood up and stepped off the ledge. Any observer having the ability to see the spiritual world at that moment would have seen the Messenger standing in mid-air, the street twenty floors below. "What do you want, Deama?"

The Shade walked over to the ledge and stepped off. "The same thing I always want, Death Dealer - your blood at my feet. Your head on a stick."

The Messenger pulled the long dagger from his coat as the rain began to fall. "If you think you can take it, Shade, I am here."

The demon looked up into the grey sky and adjusted his glasses. "You know, I could have killed him in France. I was a doctor then. I had the opportunity to kill a lot of them. Lambs to the slaughter."

The Messenger scanned the sky, looking for an ambush. "Why didn't you, Shade? Why not take the chance when you had it?"

The demon thought for a moment. "I'm not really sure. Maybe it was too easy. You know, I like a challenge. You do know that I got his father?" The Shade chuckled without humor. "Son-of-a-bitch never saw it coming. Oh, the wailing and weeping for that one. That was well worth the effort. Got the whole family shook up. Shit, some of them even blame the old man for his death - priceless."

The Messenger made no attempt to hide his weapon. "What do want, Deama? I am tired of listening to you."

"I don't want anything from you, Death Dealer. Just wanted you to know that we took it easy on your boy. We didn't think he was worth too much of an effort. Still don't."

"You were beaten, Shade. You lost thousands, maybe more. I would say that was a concerted effort."

The demon turned and walked back across the gap to the edge of the roof. "We'll get thousands more; reinforcements are not a problem now a days," he replied over his shoulder. "They can't join the ranks fast enough. Is this a great world or what? Easy pickings."

"It will be great when all of your kind are destroyed and gone," replied the Messenger. "Then things will be great. You're nothing but a plague. You should have been destroyed when you were thrown out."

The Shade stopped and laughed. "Your side has been saying that for ten thousand years, Slave. Oh, total, destruction - I'm all a quiver. You should know better." He walked off laughing and then disappeared into thin air, leaving the foul smell of decayed death behind.

The Messenger placed the dagger back in its sheath, conflicted as to why he did not kill the Shade on sight. He should have taken his head the moment they met. He walked back to the ledge and sat down, realizing that by not ending the Shade, he was prolonging the suffering of others, probably many.

What he was sure of though is that Mike would want an answer. Since the Fall, there was to be no quarter given to the outcasts, none. Violations to this command would be dealt with severely. Once in the ranks of the Legion, one had tremendous power. With that power came tremendous responsibility, responsibility never to be taken lightly.

Other Messengers who had been swayed by the Shade spent centuries chained in darkness, a fate he did not want to share. A low peel of thunder rolled across the city as the streetlights below started to blink on. No, from now on he would be extra diligent in his duties, a strict adherence to the code. As he drifted down to street level, he waited until he was sure he would not be seen before suddenly appearing in their reality. He would not take anymore unnecessary chances. The stakes were far too high.

***

On the evening of June 23,1918, the British built, three-hundred-foot steamship, HMY Alexandra, slipped quietly from her harbor moorings. Moving slowly through a calm sea and a clear night, it was a good start to a peaceful voyage. A hundred and sixteen wounded American soldiers had been loaded on board earlier that day and were now settled in for the ten-day journey from the harbor at Brest, France, to New York. Most would survive the trip. The more seriously wounded would stay in Paris until they were able to travel with some certainty of survival. There were four attending physicians and a handful of nurses onboard the Alexandra, a British ship converted into a floating hospital in the early part of the war. They would do everything they could for the injured passengers. Staterooms had been turned into stuffy, crowded wards with patients stacked two bunks high. The cots were numbered and organized within the room with regard to the severity of the occupants' injuries. Those who could walk or at least hobble to the galley for regular mess bunked in the front of the ward. Those unable to walk, like the soldier in cot number 17, would have their food brought to them.

"Here you go, Private. Dinner." The nurse handed the soldier the metal tray.

"Ma'am, I'm not real hungry right now. Maybe you could give it to some other fella."

The heavyset nurse read the nametag attached to the bunk railing. "Well, you may not be hungry, Private Jonathon Howard, but my orders are to see that you eat, which is what you will do. We have ten days to get you healthy enough to walk off this ship, and I intend to do everything in my power to make that happen." She reached in her apron pocket and pulled out a metal fork. "You will need this, Private. Eat."

Jonathon took the fork. "Yes, Ma'am. Ah, Ma'am, can I talk to you a minute?"

The nurse wiped her hands on her apron. "You have to be quick, Private. I have other men that need to be fed."

"Yes, Ma'am. It's just that I don't know how I got here. I don't know what happened to me."

The nurse glanced at the large bandages covering his shoulder and hip. "Looks like you've been shot, twice, by the looks of it. And you have a pretty good scar on your face. You don't remember getting any of that?"

He thought for a moment as scattered images flashed through his mind.

"Private, you really don't remember how you were injured?"

"Ah, maybe a little, but how did I get here? This is a ship. Right?"

The nurse smiled, patting him on the wrist, "They carried you on this afternoon, Private. Now, eat your dinner. I'll come back for the tray in a bit."

"Yes, ma'am. Ah, nurse....."

"Private?"

"Why can't I remember anything?"

The nurse thought for a moment, her face clouded with melancholy. "Well, maybe there are some things in this war we shouldn't remember. By the looks of those bandages, Private, I'd say forgetting is a blessing."

Jonathon nodded as several more images played out in blood-colored detail in his mind, the stuff of dreams, the sharp edged fragments of nightmares. "Yes, Ma'am. Maybe you're right."

The nurse smiled. "I'll check on you later, Private. You'll be fine." Before she left the room, she turned with an odd smile. "You know, Jonathon, you've earned your place. Well done."

In stunned silence, he sat staring at the empty doorway letting a memory of another time and another place wash over him, a place of unspeakable beauty and unimaginable danger. Both memories rolled themselves into a heart-splitting emotion that brought tears and a smile. Tears, for what was lost, and a smile, from the soul, for what was found. He would be home in ten days and his life would start again. There would be no regrets. He would live the rest of his life on earth with a clear vision of who he was, acutely aware of how his choices could and would determine the future, his future. He had been given a second chance, a chance that few rarely receive - truly a gift from God.

By midnight, the Alexandra was cutting a clean wake through the black waters of the cold Atlantic, carrying the timid hopes and fragmented dreams of men who had all "earned their place". The "War to end all Wars" had taken so much from so many. For others, it seeded the future with a chance of not repeating the mistakes of the past. History would be the judge.

With ships, as it is with men, cruel fate and irony sometimes come together. That would be the case with the Alexandra. On June 9th, 1940, twenty-two years after initial service as a hospital ship in France, she was discovered off the coast of Norway by a patrol of German fighter aircraft. After a valiant effort, running at full speed and an hour of desperate evasive maneuvers, she was strafed, set ablaze, and sent to the bottom of the North Atlantic.

Chapter Seventeen

They had left Fresno the day before, headed east. The drive had been easy. Even in the towns of Needles and Barstow, where the temperatures can easily get into the triple digits by early spring, the heat was mild. They had gone to California the week before to see his parents, a road trip that they both needed.

"There's a museum I kind of want to stop at. It's in Fallon, off highway Fifty. Okay? It's not far off our route."

Danielle checked Map-quest. "What's it called?"

"It's called the Fallon Navel Air Station Museum. It has some pretty cool planes I'd like to check out. It won't take long, I promise."

Danielle found the listing. "Yeah, I found it. We've got about sixty miles to the turn-off. Airplanes, huh? Didn't think you were in to that kind of thing."

"Hey, Sweetie, there're a lot of things you don't know about Craig Dawson. For all you know I might be an 'International Man of Mystery'."

Danielle laughed while putting her bare feet up on the dashboard. "I know. You hard core insurance guys are hip deep in all kinds of special operations - profit and loss statements, risk analyses, all white-knuckle stuff if you ask me."

He smiled while lowering his sunglasses. "You bet your ass, baby. Danger is my middle name."

It had been five years since Jim had died, five years of trying to heal the open wound in her heart for the man she loved more than any other. Craig had been there through it all. He and Jim had been friends for years. When Craig's wife had died years ago from cancer, Jim had been there for fishing trips, hunting trips, and just hanging out, the kind of guy-stuff that helped a man get through that kind of pain. Then, when Jim died, Craig had made it a point to help her out anyway he could, making sure there was nothing romantic between them. He handled all the life insurance matters, having been their Agent for years. He had steered her to a competent probate attorney so she wouldn't lose the house or get nailed by taxes. A year ago, after a slow courtship that had led to love, they married. Both were tired of being alone and recognized that second chances for happiness don't come by every day, especially for widowers beyond their fifties. At that age, you don't question why good things happen; you're just grateful that they still do.

This was their first long trip together, which had been a genuine joy for both of them. He had always admired Danielle, her faith and her strength, both tested to the limit with Jim's sudden death. The trip to see his parents in California had only solidified in his mind that the two were a good match. He recognized that he was falling in love with her more each day.

An hour later they spotted the Fallon Navel Air Station sign just off Highway Eighty and made the turn. It was late in the afternoon when they pulled into the visitor's area parking lot right in front of a World War II, B-24 bomber. "Pretty cool, huh?" he said, turning off the ignition. "Read about this place on *Things to Do in Nevada*. Ready to go look at some airplanes?"

Danielle laughed while opening the door. "Hey, I am on vacation. I don't need to be back at the hospital for a week. Let's go." They walked slowly across the nearly vacant parking lot, checking out several other World War II aircraft. At the far end of the gravel lot stood a huge modern hanger with a large "Visitor Center" sign posted out front. They were both struck by how few people were there. In fact, they were apparently the only visitors in the entire complex.

They stepped through the building's heavily tinted glass door into an expansive, brightly-lit hanger. Craig let out a slow whistle. "Wow, look at this!" Inside, under the bright overhead floodlights were at least ten fully restored military aircraft, everything from two magnificent Douglas A-4B Sky Hawks, a Grumman A-6 E Intruder, to an array of lethal-looking Soviet Migs, an amazing display of military hardware.

"Howdy folks." They turned to the voice, spotting an approaching heavier-set man dressed in a tight, khaki jumpsuit. Well into his sixties, he had a familiar presence of many other Military retirees - men proud to be associated with the service who held onto that pride long after the military had left them behind. They were the volunteers and the caretakers for countless places like this - guardians of the ghosts. "You folks visitors?" he asked smiling.

"Yes, Sir, " replied Craig shaking hands. "Really a cool set up you have here."

"Well, thank you. We're very proud of the aircraft we have. I'm Chet by the way, and your name, ma'am?"

"Danielle," she replied, smiling.

"Pleasure. Say would you folks mind signing in? We like to keep track of the number of people who stop by."

"Absolutely," replied Craig. "Where do we sign?"

"Great. Over here, folks." Chet led the way to the far side of the building to a small desk. They both signed in, noticing that there were only two other names on the log. To Danielle, it was sad that more people didn't come by.

"Where you folks from?" asked Chet, pulling up a metal chair behind the desk. To Danielle, his friendliness seemed to be a cover for loneliness, something she had seen in many men Chet's age.

"Detroit. What about you? Where you from, Chet?"

The older man smiled. "Oh, all over, young lady. My wife and I settled here a few years ago after I retired from the Navy. Said she wanted to live someplace dry and warm. Well, this is about as dry as you can get. So here we are."

Craig picked up one of the museum pamphlets. "Mind If I start looking around?"

Chet laughed. "Ah, here I go again. You folks came here to see some fine airplanes, not hear some old salt blabber away. Sorry about that."

Danielle smiled. "That's not true, Chet. If you have time, I would love it if you would show us around. I'm sure you have forgotten more about these airplanes than most people ever know."

Chet was now blushing, which was just the effect she was looking for. "Well, Danielle, I would be happy to. I flew just about everything in here for twenty years when I was on active duty. Follow me, and we will start at the back of the hanger. Got a whole new group of things in just last week that I think you'll like."

Danielle was right. As they moved from plane to plane, Chet seemed to have an infinite knowledge concerning every aircraft on display. His face and manner came alive as he talked about the different features and capabilities of each one. After a solid forty-five minutes, he led them over to a large display of framed black and white photographs on the hanger wall.

"These are pictures that have been donated by different people over the years. It's broken down into sections: World War I, World War II, Vietnam, and then the Gulf Wars on the end. Some of these pictures have captions on them. Some of them don't."

"Are all of them aircraft related?" asked Craig, leaning in to get a closer look at one of the pictures.

"No, not all. If it's military related, we take 'em and put them on the wall. A good example is this group of World War I pictures down here. We just got those in. Those were found in some estate sale out in Carson City. It was a couple that had come out here from back East, years ago. Rumor has it that the old man that died back in the seventies is in one of those pictures, lived to be about ninety. The last name is Howard. At least I think that's the name in the donation book."

Danielle walked down to the end of the display where several of the new eight-by-ten black and white photos had been hung. The light above the array of photos had been installed professionally, illuminating the pictures perfectly. She slowly walked by the photos studying the youthful faces of the men pictured sitting around World War I tanks, broken fields of barbed wire on the edges of mud-filled trenches. In every picture, the men appeared dirty, tired, and in some cases, terribly sad. Their crushing fatigue and fear came through their eyes, even though many of them sat with other comrades bristling with weaponry. War had marked them deeply. Walking by one of the photos, she suddenly stopped, her heart skipping a beat as she leaned in close to get a better look. The cracked and yellowed, scotch-taped caption read *Marines at Bella Wood France, 1918"*

"Chet, where did you say this picture came from?" she asked, feeling as if she were about to pass out.

"Ah, like I said, those came from that estate sale last week. I wasn't here when they dropped them off."

Danielle let the tears fall as she looked over at Craig. "Honey, come here please."

Alarmed by her change in behavior, he quickly walked over. "What's wrong, sweetie?"

Trembling while looking at the photo, she pointed to the picture as more tears fell. "Look."

He leaned in close and was stunned speechless by what he saw. There were three Marines in full, World War I battle-gear sitting on the edge of a muddy trench. Evidently the photo had been taken by one of the many professional war photographers working throughout the war. Of the three Marines, the one in the middle was holding an odd gaze directly toward the camera. It was a face Craig immediately knew. Shocked, he looked at Danielle, who was now sobbing softly. "This, this can't be," he said looking back at the photo. "It just can't."

Danielle nodded, sniffing back tears. "It's him, Craig. I swear to God, it's Jim."

"Sweetie, calm down. This picture was taken in 1918. How could that possibly be Jim? It's just someone who looks like him. C'mon, Sweetheart, don't be upset. It's just an old picture."

She looked back at the picture shaking her head. "Craig, I lived with the man for ten years. I don't know how or why he is in the photo, but it's him."

"You folks okay?" asked Chet walking up. "Anything I can do?"

Danielle smiled through the tears. "We're fine, Chet. I just saw someone in the picture that reminded me of someone I knew. I'm Okay. Really, just took me by surprise, that's all."

Craig nodded, putting his arm around her shoulders. "C'mon, Slugger. Let's go. Thank you, Chet. Thanks for the tour."

"Gosh, folks, hope everything is all right."

Craig smiled, handing him a fifty-dollar bill. "I saw that you take donations, Chet. Go ahead and put this in the jar. And thanks again. She's just tired."

Danielle was grateful it was dark as they drove out of the parking lot. She knew she probably looked a mess with her puffy eyes and smeared makeup. Seeing Jim's face had brought it all back - the fear, the confusion and the anger. She had railed against God for years about the perceived injustice of it all.

Strangely enough, upon reflection, she recognized she had an odd kind of peace, an indefinable sense that Jim was all right, and most importantly, that he had been all right all along. With no other explanation she could think of for the feeling, she rested in her heart, knowing for the first time that he had been given a second chance. God, in his infinite mercy had done something extraordinary, and she had been allowed to realize it.

As he drove, Craig looked over and patted her hand. "Sweetheart, are you okay?"

She rolled down the window letting the warm desert air blow through her hair, drying her eyes, calming her soul. The wild scent of sage made her smile as the last bit of sun disappeared in the west behind them. "I'm fine, baby. I'm fine. Just drive."

THE END

EPILOGE:

He who dwells in the shelter of the most high will abide in the shadow of the Almighty. I will say to the Lord, "He is my refuge and my fortress, my God, in whom I trust."

For, he will deliver you from the snare of the fowler and from deadly pestilence. He will cover you with his pinions and under his wings you will find refuge. His faithfulness is a shield and buckler.

You will not fear the terror of the night, nor the arrow that flies by day, nor the pestilence that stalks in darkness, nor the destruction that stalks at noonday, A thousand my fall at your side, ten thousand at your right hand but it will not come near to you.

PSALM 91....

"Cast a cold eye on life, on death, horseman pass by".

WB Yeats.

Acknowledgements:

I would like to thank Linda Clark for her vital support and encouragement in my journey to be a better writer.

As with all my work, none of it would be possible without the tireless patience, love, and emotional support of my wife, Terri. For this I am most humbly grateful.

Made in the USA
Lexington, KY
30 January 2017